THE
FIREBUGS

THE
FIREBUGS

Peter Faecke

Translated from the German by
ARNOLD J. POMERANS

19   66

ALFRED · A · KNOPF
New York

L. C. catalog card number: 65-11108

THIS IS A BORZOI BOOK,
PUBLISHED BY ALFRED A. KNOPF, INC.

FIRST AMERICAN EDITION

Originally published in German under the title *Die Brand-
stifter*. © 1963 by Walter-Verlag AG, Olten and Freiburg
im Breisgau.

THE
FIREBUGS

U P FLEW the pigeon. As their footsteps grew louder it swept low across the street and settled on a television aerial. They paused at the prison fence. Then they heard it again—the sound that had made them abandon their game of hopscotch—a muffled scraping and clattering, like stone striking stone. They were near enough to the barred window now to hear soft sounds of gurgling laughter above the sporadic clatter. The three of them stood listening for a while. Then one of the boys linked his hands and helped the girl up. Behind the fence, the prison wall rose, a sheer twelve feet of crumbling stucco, to a row of barred windows; among the trampled pansies at its foot lay stones and lumps of clay embossed by heavy boots, and around the window towards which the girl was now groping, the plaster

5

bore grimy scars—witnesses to yesterday's mob. Can you see him? asked the boy shifting his grip to the girl's ankles.

Not yet.

Well, come down. I can't hold you.

She strained to reach the window and locate the gurgling sound.

Leave it, you're shaking all over, he said.

No, wait.

And balancing her heels on his palms she now placed her toes on the fence while the other boy stared up her legs. Just then the noises stopped: a moment's silence broken only by the cooing of the pigeon on the television aerial. Then the muffled sound of near-by Gindenhall—a hooter, faint footsteps, the brittle stroke of a clock, quarter past. Gradually the gurgling started up again.

Is he there? Can you see him?

Gurgling laughter echoing through a barred window, as the girl groped, reached, paused, peered, and at last saw a man in a torn shirt, crouching motionless on his bed, head between jean-clad thighs. A strand of yellow hair was stuck to his quavering mouth. The girl held her breath. Perhaps Hawe felt something blocking the light, or else he saw the shadow of her head pressed tight for added support against the bars;

6

in any case, he sat up suddenly, stopped his gurgles, and stared at her with the eyes of an idiot. She jerked her face back from the bars.

What's happened? Have you seen him?

She clung a moment longer to the battered wall, groped with her foot for the boy's hand, and jumped off the fence, panting but saying nothing, and filled with the kind of confused excitement that follows a slap in the face.

But you don't even know the town, so how can you possibly understand Hawe from what I have told you about a startled pigeon and a frightened little girl? Perhaps I had better start a day earlier, at the office. It was Pnip's last day. From his desk he could see the church clock showing five, but not striking for a few minutes and then splitting the sultry September air. At last it was a quarter past, a solitary trembling of the bell, and Pnip cleared his desk before leaving. The door swung to behind him, revealing the legend C. BOETTCHER—IMPORT & EXPORT in ornamental copper lettering. It was the last time Pnip was to join the drift of bicycles, scooters, three-wheelers and Volkswagens towards the Old Town. There he turned off, rode along the banks of the Este, past houses that rushed towards him and then swung back to reveal the allotments on the fringe of the town.

7

That evening, Uncle Pomsig's toolshed could be spotted from far away, with the sun's copper glow catching its top window. As Pnip turned into the sandy drive, the glow disappeared, and all that was left of the sun's light, like ashes after a blaze, was a pale reflection from the lime-coloured boards and the dull-black roofing felt.

Clara watched him pass and then enter without a greeting. Her tired voice said coldly and pointlessly, as always: Your food is in the larder. He sat down on the edge of the bed, pulled up the table, took the lid off the stew-pot, and removed the towel and paper which were keeping the cabbages and potatoes hot. All this time she stood motionless at the window. He saw her from the bed, or rather he observed her. The greying hair, scraped back into a bun, looked transparent in the twilight; beneath it, a faded lace collar and black dress accentuated the stiff back she had turned on him. Then he noticed that she too, was watching: the window pane threw back his neatly-parted hair, slightly uptilted nose and half-open mouth, side by side with her steel-rimmed spectacles —two faces set in glass. For a while they just looked at each other.

Well, what is it? she said at last in a dull voice, not losing sight of his reflection for an instant.

Nothing. He made a desultory attempt to swallow the food.

You might as well tell me.

There's nothing to tell.

What do you mean, nothing?

It's only . . . oh, who the hell cares, anyway.

Go on.

It's just that you've been lying to me. God knows for how many years too. And all that time it never even occurred to me that you weren't my mother.

Clara still did not move. She remained at the window, her slight silhouette and head imperceptibly tilted towards the spot where she could watch him seated on the bed.

I suppose someone has been talking, she said, but by then the table had been pushed back, and while she remained at the window, Pnip had stepped out into the evening air, walked towards the garage, and was now riding down the drive past the redcurrant bushes. As he opened the throttle along the Ginden-hall road, the air rushed past him, lapping against his face and body like the sea. Clara waited at the window until he had left the estate.

When he reached the edge of the town, he suddenly braked, swerved towards the Este, and bounced to its edge over furrows and molehills. Here swarms

9

of midges hung like clusters of grapes in the still air above the stone jetty. He jumped off his scooter, crouched over the water and sought his reflection. Then he leant back to watch the midges' intricate patterns, and the water lapping softly against the wall in front of him. This must have been the place. He suddenly needed its certainty. Yes, this was it, this very spot. Even now he could recall the sniggers of little Hans Weinrich, with his never-ending dares, until in the end he had taken the cat across. How many years ago was it, how many years had Clara been lying to him, and he believing her all the time, yes, even here at the Este? And Hans Weinrich had bolted, afraid of the scratches. And big Magosch and Rolf Schrader having to wipe the blood off their legs and chests, for the cat had given as good as it got. The swarm of midges came closer, drifted into his line of vision, and flicked away again. . . . And Rolf Schrader was still wiping the red ooze from his chest, when Pnip finally climbed out of the water after twice crossing the Este without getting a single scratch. He had won.

Above the swarm he could just make out the tower of St. Blasius, a dark form that would merge into night within the hour. Was it not within sight of this same tower, in this same stale evening air, perhaps

10

this very place, that, lazing in the sun with big Magosch, Hans Weinrich and Rolf Schrader, he had first set eyes on Erna?—Again he bent over the water. His reflection disintegrated into drifting parts, the neatly combed hair, uptilted nose and broad cheek-bones. But the ripples could not destroy the pasty complexion that Hans Weinrich and all the others had jeered at before this business with the cat. For he had been the only one whose legs and chest were not covered with red smears, he whom they had always thought a weed with his white face, queer name, and tired smile—his only answer to their taunts of Pnipsqueak and Riffraffugee. From then on they all started to copy him. They were even more impressed by the cool way in which he handed in two blank sheets after a history test; he should have written on Alexander's unification of East and West but he disliked the subject. And then, just as coolly, he sailed through his Latin and Maths getting full marks as if trying to prove that it could be done without pleasure or effort, and ambition, as everyone knew, did not come into it.

One day he no longer wore the blue polo-neck sweater in which they knew him, and appeared in a white shirt and neat tie. After P.T. he stood in front of the looking-glass, adjusted his tie, snapped his

11

cuff links shut, and smoothed his collar—and all these gestures without a trace of vanity. Even when the looking-glass was dirty—someone must have rubbed mud on it—and he used a pocket mirror, Pierke, Magosch, and Schrader still did not think him vain. But though no one realized that the tie, and cuff links, like his smile, were a deliberate pose, they knew something must have happened to their Pnip-squeak. And just as they used to imitate his expression and his odd way of lounging about, so two or three of them now appeared in ties. But then Pnip gave up wearing ties again, and all of the others dropped theirs like scabs. He was not at all concerned with setting a new trend or with the pride of invention; all he intended with his collar and tie, his neatly parted hair, his smile, or if you prefer, his resigned grimace that looked like a kind of smile, was to keep his distance. Wounded by their taunts of Pnipsqueak and Riffraffugee or even by just having to share a classroom with them, he sought reassurance from his own image in the glass. And when he failed to get it, he made sure of his identity by wreathing his blurred image in a deliberate flourish of his own, a kind of hallmark, something he alone possessed, that helped him to make up for his outlandish name, and to bear their parents' questions of:

What's your friend's name?

Pnip.

No, his real name.

That is his real name. Pnip.

Pnip what?

Just Pnip.

Anyway, that's what happened when Hans Weinrich, the teacher's son, first asked him home, and took him and Magosch up to the attic. Frau Weinrich, blonde and forever fluttering her blue eyelids like a hen, called up to them—You will be good won't you Hans?—and he promised. The attic had been white-washed and beneath the plaster you could still see the beams which an earlier Weinrich, no doubt a teacher too, had used to build the house.

Do you know how my grandfather finished up? Weinrich asked, but Pnip had already moved to the table under the window—to the train set.

It's a Maerklin, Weinrich said. Surely you don't still play with things like that? But all Pnip said was—Where is the plug, and how does the control box work? He also asked to switch it on, and if it really was all right for him to play with the set. Weinrich sniggered but showed him how to work it. So there was Pnip playing with trains when what they had really come up for was Weinrich's 'trophies' as

Magosch called them with a knowing grin. Pnip coupled two Shell tankers to an engine. Then, starting a passenger train back at the station, he sent it past the green signal and over two points into the plastic tunnel, and through the village. Just in front of the level crossing was a loose contact; the train stopped and had to be given a slight push before continuing into the long loop at the corner of the room. What on earth are you doing? Magosch called. Stop messing about, for Christ's sake! But Pnip merely sent the tankers off, having first added three refrigerator trucks. Can't you just see him crouching under the window, perhaps still smiling to himself, but in any case bent over the control box, directing the passenger train and now speeding the tankers round the loop into the plastic tunnel. God Almighty, it was understandable enough, he had never owned a train set in his life.

Look here, Weinrich protested, I thought you wanted to see my things. Well are you going to or not?

He's much too young, Magosch sneered.

Weinrich shrugged his shoulders and walked across the attic. An old cane chair and a chest stood near the chimney; on the floor lay several old mattresses, the remains of a bicycle, and a pedal car. Here where the roof sagged, the tiles had shifted a little and dust

14

floated up in the sunbeams. The Este sounded unreal
and far away. Suddenly a door slammed downstairs.
That's my old man, but he doesn't know a thing,
Weinrich said. He pushed one of the mattresses aside
and forced his penknife between the floor boards,
prised one up, grasped it with his left hand and lifted
it out. Magosch leant forward in anticipation. First
Weinrich produced an old kitchen towel and then,
rooting further in, a parcel.

Let's start with Aunt Faesschen, shall we? he said.
He rummaged eagerly in the parcel, paused dramati-
cally and came up with an embroidered garter of
indecent proportions. Dangling it in front of him he
got up, threw back his head, and danced a little jig.
Magosch exploded with laughter, jabbed a hand
into his pocket and nudged Pnip.

That's really something, isn't it? I bet you have never
seen one like it! And it came straight off Aunt
Faesschen.

She was the fat old girl downstairs, Weinrich
explained.

He was crouched over the parcel again, digging away
in it for all he was worth. Then he noticed that
Magosch, hand in trouser pocket still, had gone red
in the face, and he burst out laughing. They had to
bring her down to the living room, Weinrich said,

and Hanne and I weren't allowed in any more. They told us she was going abroad as if we would be fool enough to believe them, when the old man had been saying all the time: No man in his right senses would look twice at that old hag. Take it from me, she's here for keeps. But she kept buying frilly things and getting fatter all the time, what with lying in bed and stuffing her face with chocolates. She didn't mind us sneaking in, though, and helping ourselves, so long as we kept away from her cupboard. As if we didn't know all about the baby things inside, and about her buying more every spring and counting them over all the time. I would often see them in the mirror, as she stood in her nightie plaiting her hair while the cupboard was wide open. Christ Almighty, she would yell, spying on me again, and slam the door shut and lock the cupboard.

You dirty bastard, Magosch said with mock indignation, scratching his groin.

It had become very hot in the attic, the sounds of the Este and the town seemed more muffled still and yet even closer.

But we got the stuff in the end, Weinrich added. When she couldn't get down to the lav any more and they had to move her to the living room. That's when I had a go at her cupboard with my penknife.

16

Did you always watch her from the door? said Magosch.

Where the hell can she have put it, I said to myself, and then I saw this mountain of lace, the bloody cupboard stuffed full with it, and I pulled the whole lot out and dragged it into the garden. And all the time, she was feeling perfectly safe with that damned cupboard key tied round her fat neck. What's the matter with you today, he said to Magosch.

In reply Magosch put his hand down his shirt front and pulled up two French letters.

Is that the best you could do?

Go to hell, I pinched the goddam things.

Well, it's not good enough. Last time it was a lousy candle. Bet it came off a Christmas tree.

Now look here, snarled Magosch—you could see he was furious—let me tell you. . .

Well?

Give me back the gun, then. Did I get that off a Christmas tree too; or bought it from the Yanks, maybe? You know bloody well I stole the bastard. So what?

And that old steel helmet from the grave in the Questenberg—and those Chesterfields.

All right. You win.

Well, shut your mouth then, said Magosch.

17

But what about Pnip, Weinrich interrupted. What's he got to offer?

Me?

Yes, you.

Oh, nothing, said Pnip. He had been leaning against the chimney, watching Weinrich unwrap the parcel and Magosch rummaging in his pockets. No, nothing—he repeated with that same apologetic little smile.

Nothing, eh?

He's just an outsider, said Magosch, still furious—so what can you expect?

Oh shut up. Let him bring something later.

So it was agreed, and Pnip was allowed to come out into the garden with them. As they passed Mrs. Weinrich, she asked why Pnip was leaving so soon. She addressed Pnip as 'Mr. Pnip', fluttering her eyelids so much that Weinrich and Magosch had to giggle.

Grandfather Weinrich had planted the fruit trees as well. Even that rusty iron fence was his handiwork, boasted Weinrich. That's his picture in the living room over Auntie Faesschen's couch. It must have been in Bismarck's time, when our school was first opened.

The hide-out was among the roots of a willow tree

18

and screened from the house by other trees and bushes. Stamped clay provided a floor beneath the moss-festooned roof boards. Weinrich produced a long American cigarette. The smoke rose through a tube fixed to the willow stem so that it couldn't be seen from the house. It hung in the air like cotton wool, then disappeared. Again they talked of Grandfather Weinrich. You mean to say, you never heard of Bismarck? Anyway it was about that time. Grandad must have been an old rake with his big whiskers, just feel the edge of his sword. But Magosch refused; he had seen it all before and in any case he had just come across the revolver.

Suddenly Adolf Weinrich began to roar from the house, cursing his son for leaving Hanne behind and for making her cry. Magosch and Pnip took to their heels.

They paused and said: see you sometime; then Pnip went back to the allotments. The whole place looked cramped and mean; all the trees did was undermine the foundations, and who wanted all those miserable greens anyway. Birds fluttered from the hedgerows as Pnip passed.

Only in the changing room did the other boys notice. Lieneck was whistling and shouting for them to fall in smartly and to start the exercise. Pnip took off his

19

shirt and the cry went up—Look, Pnip's turned into a girl.

Sneeringly they gathered round and Fuchs grabbed the chain that hung from his neck. It caught the light and the others bent eagerly forward expecting to see a Madonna at least; but what Fuchs read out was: Greetings from Gindenhall. The thing was made of brass and couldn't have cost more than one mark twenty in the souvenir shop under the Este bridge. When Pnip raised his knee, it dangled from his neck; and when he bent forward it swung into his face. Fuchs, who was meant to support Pnip in the exercises, suddenly clutched the chain once more and prised the clasp open. Pnip stopped work and went after him, but the chain was now travelling with Magosch across the wall bars and out on to the beams. Beyond the windows it was passed to Pierke who hesitated when he saw that Pnip had returned to his exercises; then he slid down the rope. Now Lieneck had seen it. A whistle blast brought Magosch and the others down from the wall bars. Pnip stopped his knee bends when Pierke jumped off the rope and gave the chain to the sports master. Pnip's sad smile showed only weariness. All around them was the stink of chalk and sweat.

Lieneck took the chain from Pierke and read aloud—

Greetings from Gindenhall—What will you think up next, you can collect it from the office later, he said and a whistle blast sent them scampering back to their positions. Pierke funked it, so they all waited for Pnip to go for the chain. Wait until after the English lesson he told them—then all he said was—I'm going. He returned from the office a few minutes later with two shirt buttons undone. No sign of emotion; just that open shirt—but they knew he must have seen the secretary upstairs, perhaps even the headmaster. And he had done it where Pierke had been too scared. They all stopped sneering at him after that.

Schrader was the first to visit the souvenir shop under the bridge, clutching his one mark twenty for a chain. A boy in one of the lower classes went next, until even Magosch sported one. When that happened, Pnip abandoned the whole thing, and searched again for something that would be his alone.

So it came about that when they were all wearing jeans, crew cuts, and sunglasses, he had the idea of wearing sandals. Their quest for coloured fragments of glass in the river by the glassworks had resulted in cut feet; Pierke, the butcher's son, had been the first. The following day they all came from town with galoshes and gym shoes tied to their handlebars. At first Pnip wore linen slippers when he went into the water, but one day he appeared in a pair of ornate sandals which had cost him eighteen marks, earned from private lessons. Nobody could copy him at that price, so, at last, he had something truly his own. Even Pierke could only manage a pair of white plastic bathing slippers which paled into insignificance next to Pnip's. And while Pierke was still struggling to stain his slippers with brown wax and having trouble with the rusty buckles, Pnip was again wearing ordinary shoes. It was not their attempts at imitation but his own boredom with it that exhausted the disguise.

True, Weinrich put it down to the protruding big toe. It sometimes struck the kerbstone when Pnip crossed the street and left a fine trail of red droplets. In any case he stopped wearing sandals in the middle of summer. Once again all he was left with was that enigmatic smile, the twist of the mouth that served as a smile.

Autumn brought an occasional revival of the tie and a whole gallery of peculiar studs, but nothing they could really have imitated. This went on until shortly before the summer term ended, when he lay gasping across Hans Weinrich. For a moment it seemed he would attack Magosch as well. But all I really know of this is the obvious: his tie, the stiff collar, the

expensive sandals and their nicknames for him—
and none of it was really essential. But it was different with Erna. The boys used to go down to the Este
in the afternoons, leaping and chasing into the water,
hanging on to the Bremen barges and even trying
to clamber aboard until the swinging slop bucket
drove them back. It was their last year at the Gott-
lieb-Fichte Gymnasium and Pnip had suddenly
changed. Their only defence against his smile had
been to boast about their girl friends, for they had
never seen him with one. But that day he was
wrestling with Weinrich in the grass over a girl and
got the better of him. She stood upriver in a haze of
sunlight. Behind her Pnip could see the tower of St.
Blasius, and the roofs of the old city; not in the
present amber glow of evening but sharp in the harsh
afternoon light, her figure framed as in a shop
window. She seemed close enough to touch.

Boy, oh boy. Give anything to lay her, I would,
whispered Weinrich.

Shut up, said Pnip.

Poised on his elbows, he watched the girl. Then, with
a curse, he snatched an ant from his groin, held it up
for inspection in the sunlight, and squashed it between thumb and finger.

Come on, let's try her.

23

Leave her alone, can't you.

I bet she'd like it just as much as we would.

Weinrich jumped up and started waving to the girl, but Pnip launched himself against his legs and dragged him to the ground. They struggled in the grass until Weinrich broke free, fell, and then scrambled away under Pnip's arm and across the grass. But Pnip had caught him again and pinioned him down. He wrenched Weinrich's freckled face towards him and raised his fist. Magosch suddenly laughed. He had watched the contest sitting cross-legged on his robe. Now he laughed. Pnip let go of Weinrich and lay gasping in the grass.

It's only Erna Blume, Magosch said, that old elephant legs from Moslau who still jibbers away in Polish or something. Once again he laughed.

Pnip glared at Magosch who braced himself for the attack. But Pnip started smiling at him. Gathering his clothes together he tied them to the bicycle. The others were laughing now and rolling in the grass, though their forced laughter could not blot out the image of Pnip in anger. Something had stopped him, perhaps a memory of something they could never share. While they had revelled in the fight and hoped they could goad him further, he had stopped and smiled that same smile that had aroused their hostility

24

and that they all tried to copy later on. First Pierke, then Schrader and finally even Magosch, with the youthful uncertainty of trying on new expressions like gloves.

Do you think it was the 'elephant legs' that did it?

Yes,—no, I don't know what's eating him.

Next day Weinrich and Magosch were back in the same place (here, where Pnip was now watching his face in the midge-shrouded river). Perhaps a bird sang, or a grasshopper chirped in the still air. Then came the sound of a bicycle bell. They sat up and saw first Pnip, then Erna, old elephant legs as Magosch had called her, turn off with a girl friend towards the Este. A blanket fluttered aloft, then all three disappeared into the grass and low bushes. Weinrich was grinning all over his face. The heat lay on the grass like snail slime. He beckoned Magosch towards the Este, bending below the screen of sun-dried stalks. When they approached the place, they started to crawl, carefully parting the grass screen before them.

Can you see them?

No, can you?

For a moment they lay panting in the bushes. Then they edged forward again. Weinrich saw the blanket first and he began to chuckle. There was Erna and her friend and in front of them was Pnip. Weinrich

25

crawled forward into the bushes, paused for a moment and then turned back indignantly.

If I hadn't seen it with my own eyes, I'd swear Pnip hadn't got one. Just look at him squatting in front of her. He doesn't have the first idea of how to do it. Like a dead duck.

Or a maybug, all popeyed.

He's just jerking it about. Twitching like a maybug and he doesn't even know what the hell is happening. Have you ever seen anything like it?

Pnip had been watching the two girls for a long time and had followed them to Moslau, waiting until they separated and Erna disappeared into one of the courtyards. Then back at the Este again, Erna, her brown hair pulled into a ponytail, had turned her oval face invitingly towards her pursuer but he had not the least idea what to do about it. She was the first, and he knew too little about the flesh or even how to simulate lust. So there he sat trembling in front of them, whilst Magosch and Hans Weinrich lay expectantly in the bushes. Just his pale face, his parted hair and his hunched shoulders. Weinrich turned away in disgust and crawled back through the dust-flecked grass.

He's lost the fucking thing or something.

Must have done.

Perhaps we ought to show him how to do it.

Just like a bloody maybug.

They crawled back to where Magosch had left his bathing robe and slithered into the water. Then they sprawled in the warmth of the sun while Pnip still squatted in the grass. Whenever the girls looked at him he would peer just over their heads with the same smile.

All was quiet but for the sound of a car on the road or perhaps a blackbird singing from a willow across the river. His image bobbed like a cork on the river, over the smell of plants, oil and weeds. The blackbird across the river flew up with the first stone. A second and then a third stone followed. His angry cast sent them high over the river before they skimmed the surface and disappeared. Then he paused arms akimbo and let the smell of the Este drift by. Perhaps he thought: if only Clara had told me herself. Just a hint would have done, or a short note. But no, she had to leave it to that bastard Hawe to tell me the truth.

The blackbird had come back again. It started singing from a bush upstream, just as Pnip jumped on his scooter and skidded past the molehills towards the town.

WELL, now you know what happened before and after the summer of '62.

I had fallen for a girl, and was anxiously waiting for the postman at Pomsig's house. But all he brought was a white square with a spindly scrawl on the back —Clara Glonski, Hasenheide 4, Gindenhall. Uncle laughed and said it was ridiculous. But that afternoon, as I was swotting away at alcohol chains, benzol, and esters—and getting nowhere—I saw him drive off all the same. He must have been curious, for it was all of seventeen years since he had seen the inside of his toolshed, since she had appeared on his verandah with the six-year-old boy demanding the place. Whenever I asked about it, he would describe her red polka-dotted scarf and her old jeans, and the way she had slammed the door in his face when he went a few days later to inspect the shed. From the beginning she had treated him in the same gruff manner, making her demands while snatching the boy away from the verandah steps where he was tugging at a juniper bush and sniffing his hand, which retained the juniper's odour of wet iron and kitchen spices. Yes, it must have been curiosity that made Pomsig drive off that afternoon, leaving me to the alcohol, the benzol and the esters. For the first time in seventeen years he would enter his toolshed in Hasenheide Street and see the woman he had tried to fob off when she had asked for the shed. It must have been in his mind later when he sat opposite her across the plastic tablecloth and listened to her fast, insistent voice. Wood crackling on the fire produced a series of small plopping explosions that echoed round the room. Curiosity and the spindly scrawl on the envelope had brought him there. So too had memories of the polka-dotted scarf, the jeans and the juniper. Until then, she had always sent the postal orders for the rent in the name of Clara Junk. What could it mean when the name on the envelope had changed from Junk to Glonski: —the name of his best client? You must be wondering why I sent for a lawyer— said Clara across the table top. Before he could answer, she continued in her even voice as if time

29

was important—You could have stayed away, of course; but you must have realized that I was sending you an S.O.S. It's an old story, not very exciting, but as Glonski's solicitor perhaps you can give the boy the help he needs during the next few days. That's what I really want; someone to help him.

Well, how on earth. . . .

Yes, I know—she broke in with her tense insistent voice, as sibilant as the spluttering firewood. He saw her spectacles glittering with a cold passivity.

You want to know how I came to sign myself Glonski, when you know me by the other name, the one I put on the postal orders. This is the first time in seventeen years that I have used it and only then to force you to come here.

I was still a young girl when Glonski gave me the ring. He came into the shop and asked Father for my hand before he had even seen me. All he cared for was that there was a marriageable daughter living in the house. Fourteen days later I accepted him, because it was the only offer I had ever had and because I would probably never get another.

Yes, I quite understand—said my uncle with patience, but she ignored him and went on talking. Uncle might have thought: There's no point in all this, she just wants to get it off her chest: all right, even if I'm a bad listener let her tell me her story. But he did try to interrupt her when he failed to see the connection between the sawmills and Glonski. As she continued in her tinny voice, he relapsed into silence, hearing the wood crackling and looking round his old tool-shed. Even as she was claiming that she had ceased ageing the moment she called herself Glonski, Uncle thought that time had petrified her as it does those who have experienced war or been close to death. Their hopes and desires become stamped upon them, hastening the decay of their bodies. Their skins become yellow and lined with age, as my uncle could now see.

Even the smell, he claimed, was like that. That embarrassing smell of old age overlaid the odour of carbolic acid and wax cloth, and the sweet scent of burning wood.

I know you are impatient, but please wait. The mouth and dark eyes behind her spectacles still retained the tiniest trace of the young girl she was describing. Under the wrinkled skin the mouth still held the promise of girlhood and her dark dreamy eyes preserved a lustre without the aid of mascara.

Ever since a quarter to five, when I saw him leave, Uncle had been listening to this woman. He was struck by her urgent yet precise pronunciation; her

31

voice filled every corner of the room as she talked of her home in Silesia. Her gestures emphasized the names—Habelschwert, Alteide, Bad Reinerz—the Czech border 700 feet above, up on the Adlerkamm. She spoke of snow-covered peaks, of feeding wild animals, and of many other things. The village was called Weisstritz and had a population of five hundred Catholics; Catholics, she repeated, but Pomsig had ceased listening. In breathless tones she urged him to imagine the two-storeyed house of Robert Junk, the grocer, the only stone building in a village full of small wooden shacks. A tall girl with long black tresses arriving every weekend from a boarding school in Glatz. The mail coach stopping at the house, then going on to the church and the school-house; who else in the village would get letters?

The girl disappearing into a house.

On the first floor above the landing crammed with sugar, flour sacks, Persil, marmalade, onions, Pilsener beer, cheap cigarettes and herrings, Anne sitting in her sitting room with her legs on a footstool.

Back again Clara; come and tell me everything, she would say and scurry around preparing the greasy plum dumplings. Whenever the door was open, the smells of the shop drifted in. Below, stood Robert Junk silently shovelling sugar into one and two pound bags to the clamour of the customers. Meanwhile Anne would watch the young girl eating. Yes, Anne did have a goitre even then. Now she began to speak quietly but firmly about the underwear. Her goitre trembled as she finally produced a set from beneath the table.

These used to be Greta's; I think it's high time you had some, too, you're growing so fast—she hesitated, then added—take them, you will be wearing them sooner or later anyway, look they are made of silk—but Clara had fled to her bedroom. Standing by the chest at the window, she lifted the lid, threw the linen in, and started to tremble. Her plaited black hair and long mournful face were visible from the street as she drew a finger across the window pane. Perhaps it was a word, even a name that she wrote —but it soon disappeared. Then she stepped back into the room, where two years later she would become the woman in black whom the villagers respectfully addressed as Teacher.

Meantime she went to the teachers' training college in Breslau and, one day when she was on her way to church, they all whispered: My goodness, what a pair she has grown—just right for it, eh?

I'll say.

Hey, Clara, shall I show you how?

Wait, you don't know what's good for you.

But she took to her heels, away from the church and from the three boys lounging in their Sunday best in front of the post office. She ran through the village, past the rhododendron bush and up the stairs lined with herring tubs and flour sacks. Her hands beat against the wall of her room until Robert Junk came upstairs and tried to console her. But the time came when it did not matter any more and she made her peace with the village. A smart accent had softened her gravelly voice when she returned home. Slender as ever, but with her braids now pinned up she would walk, in the mornings, with sharp steps up the street to her solitary classroom in the school. In the afternoons, she would take the account book and replace Anne's scrawl with her own copper-plate handwriting. Anne too had changed. And this was the time of the big drums and the storm troopers. Anne began to wear sombre clothes with a severe hair style, whilst Clara took over her old dresses. No more journeys down the valley to Campe's, clutching rolls of red and yellow material. All that was needed now was a few stitches, a tuck here, a letting-out there, or a belt round the hips. Even that became unnecessary, a two-inch seam at the hem and Anne's dresses fitted her nicely. Both of them lived increasingly on the

34

first floor of the granite house, whilst Robert Junk withdrew into the shop downstairs. It seemed that they were always together that winter—God knows which winter it was, but the drum beats were increasing then—and the following summer, too. Like two cocooned insects they hid away in the quiet seclusion of the house. No wonder the villagers began to call them 'the two sisters'. Two sisters in the same old dresses but damn it all, they were mother and daughter.

The boy was probably hunting for a crow with that catapult; Clara noticed it later in his hand. As he looked up at the roof, the snowflakes blew into his eyes, so that he had to lower them quickly. That's how he came to see his teacher behind the misty panes of the middle window. She was leaning with her forehead against the glass, eyes closed, and he noticed her mouth moving towards the glass. The lips touched, kissed and remained glued to the window pane in a misty halo. Then a snowball burst against the glass causing her to jerk back.—As you can imagine, I found an excuse for slapping him the next day at school.

My uncle had been listening to Clara. She paused a second, then began again, speaking slower now. Well that summer,—please wait a minute—all right, you want to know what the Nazis had to do with me, but please wait. One day as we were watching the arrival of the timber buyers, I saw him. He was there buying on his own account, for although he was barely twenty-four he had already managed to scrape together four sawmills. Kolczynski claimed of course that he had got it all by swindling the fire insurance. Well, that summer Anne and I grew apart again. All because of him, I dare say.

Look, I never even took his photograph out of my album—see it's still here. Well, he was leaning against a linden tree or was it a maple, I always did confuse the two. Nearby was his BMW, a common sight in our village. There was a smile on his narrow mouth but not really a smile.

See for yourself (it was like a bird's head, my uncle said later, with sleek, black hair above a smiling mask. A touch of cruelty about the mouth, emphasized by the party badge in his lapel. Under the picture was the date—June '33).

But that's only a picture; when we saw him in the flesh, we knew at once what we wanted and did not feel ashamed. In fact I knew what I wanted for the first time. We began to keep a sharp look-out for him. Here at the plantation he bought only the barest essentials and always with great care, that much

Kolczynski told us. Then off he would go, up the village street clad in those familiar plus-fours and the olive green linen jacket, which aroused curiosity every time he wore it. One day Anne followed him as far as the church. There he turned round and ambled past her with the walk of a man furtively searching for something he has lost. He must have remembered, for the next time we saw him, he kept close to the office wall and was soon screened from us by the sun blind. Something was detaining him, a chat, perhaps, or a difficult order. Father came in looking for a catalogue of spare parts or something as we were skylarking about behind the curtains.—He drives that old BMW, Kolczynski later told us as he was weeding the garden. He buys very little but what he buys is always the best. Knows what he is about, that one. Stands apart at the auction—just watching. Doesn't even drink—well the odd one here and there—but never says a word. Of course, I saw him, I was just ripping up those snowdrops, when they were still in bloom (a pity, I thought); he was crossing the road and then disappeared behind your shop blind. You could have knocked me down with a feather then. Bless me if old firebugs doesn't want to marry the girl, I said to myself, that bastard with his fancy windcheater and party badge. And her old man is too scared to say no. Not like old Stern who wouldn't even sell him a glass of beer or a box of matches. We don't need your kind here, Stern said to him.

Rhododendron blossom. The sweet rotting smell of it drifted in through the open first-floor window of the stone house. As morning passed, it clung knee high to the sun-warmed stone until stirred by a breath of wind or a chicken ruffling its feathers in one of the pens. It was summer but quite unlike this summer in Gindenhall with its brazen heat; the sky like a net forever rearranging its mesh of blue sky and pale cloud. Beneath lay the wooden roofs knotted around the church tower, all permeated by the sickly smell of rhododendron blossom. The changing pattern of the sky was reflected in Clara's mood.

That day she abandoned her forbidding black dress for a soft cream gown, and used rose-scented soap to smooth her skin. Even the severe parting had gone; she wore her hair loosely over her shoulders, a burst of flame in the sunlight. With an almost forgotten gesture she swept a lock from her forehead past her ear and pressed it slowly and gently under the slide. She looked at herself in the mirror.

Kolczynski was cleaning the ditches near the sluice gate when he heard the noise grow louder. It was the BMW climbing up the winding road and bearing

Glonski towards his bride. Kolczynski rested on his spade and watched the car curl up the hill towards him. The driver was wearing a black suit, borrowed in Bad Reinerz; across his knees a travelling rug skirted the new shoes that would receive a final polishing just outside the village. A handful of gladioli lay in the leather tool box. Kolczynski called out to him and the car came slowly to a halt.

Well, what are you up to?

Mind your own business.

Just visiting, I suppose.

And though he had only called out to him in jest, and never thought of firebugs and sawmills, Kolczynski now maintains that he recognized the face.

Tell me, friend, have you ever been in Habelschwerdt?

No.

Come now, surely that's where we first met.

As the car drew away, Kolcynski swears he saw a thin, evil smile. He might very well be, goddammit he was, the one in Habelschwerdt the morning the fire started. That shit of an arsonist who ducked away from Runger's sawmill showing just a glimpse of his back.

Clara had by then left the window at Anne's entreaty so she missed Glonski's arrival. After wiping his

39

shoes, he stuffed the rug into the tool box and marched briskly past the woodworkers' huts and the gaping inhabitants.

Do you know him?

Yes, I think so.

Can't be sure though.

Must be the one from Habelschwerdt—Kolczynski swears he saw him there.

Not even the smell of a beer does he get from me, said Stern.

Glonski must have heard it all but did not turn his head. He probably smelled the rhododendron as he strode onwards with that same purposeful step.

There goes Glonski the firebug, off to get himself a wife.

Get a bit of respectability that way.

By buying himself a pig in a poke.

Clara's voice became almost a whisper, Uncle said. Yes, the rhododendron was in blossom that summer, she went on, such a sweet smell when it entered the house. Of course I cried when it was all over.

Not until winter came did the two of them pay us a visit. From our block house I could see the car far away skidding about in the frozen ruts of the lane past the last few houses of Reinerz. It stopped and a small figure got out. Of course, I was glad, but then suddenly again all the old smells of the shop; the margarine, the sauerkraut and the herrings. The smell even brought a little of the old Clara with it. The one I had believed swept away like the very air she had breathed.

We'd have preferred you to come to us, Father said. I haven't seen you for ages.

His words were drowned by the sound of a saw or perhaps the rending crash of a falling tree. But the sounds meant nothing. Out there was Glonski, striding about in the machine shop and incessantly driving his four workers, with the same restless energy under which all my dreams had disappeared. And here was Anne looking at me with her girlish eyes. They both looked at me, demanding a confession of happiness. For a second I hated her and then Father. He took off his hat, ran his fingers through his thin hair and finally laid his hands on the table. I can still remember the way in which he clenched them into fists and drew them back under the table, as if to hide them.

Tell us, daughter, what is he like?

The steady beat of an axe. The saw rasping into the wood. And Mother's girlish eyes expecting the kind of joy in which you are oblivious to the crackle of the cheap sawdust stove and the atmosphere of hate

41

surrounding the hut. Yes, I thought, it is very easy to be decent with eyes like those. One could even bear the market and the shopping for cabbages and beetroot and eggs. It would be easy to shut out the gossip of the stallholders—that's the one from Habelschwerdt, the one the police came for. Or the one with the eggbasket, stinking of garlic.

How are the fireworks?

What?

You know, down there in Habelschwerdt.

I don't. . . .

Big fires, small fires—they all help to get workers and machines—don't they just. Even new factories, eh? Wait, love, you forgot your eggs.

I had just passed the sauerkraut and cabbage stall when something wet splashed on to the pavement, beside me. Then another splash. One whispered he actually saw the flames reflected from Glonski's face, but that they arrested a Czech in his place. For all those girlish eyes, Anne must have heard about it, too. Though she couldn't have known about the stolen trunks being unloaded at night. Or about the four men he had brought from Neukölln; with no questions asked. Glonski was always driving them like beasts as I saw whenever I brought their kümmel rations to the saw or the timber yard. Always cursing and shouting orders. You remember the photograph, of course. He barely stood still long enough even for that. Caught for a moment like a bird in flight; then off and away.

Yes, Anne knew nothing of this as she sat opposite me eagerly waiting for my confession. She had never seen the glow of firelight on his face, or heard the unloading at night. Nor did she know about the time when his sister used to pack him off to school with syrup sandwiches. Now and then he would talk about it quite coolly and with no sign of revulsion or hatred. How a dozen of them would hunt him down in their war game. How they finally caught him and thrust his face into a heap of cow dung until he was forced to gasp and swallow it down. Anne—perhaps it was really no more than a passing from one dream to the next, a brief jolt and not much more, when she learned about it three weeks later. It was a clear winter's morning when she went out and came back soon afterwards and started babbling, or so Kolczynski said: quite suddenly, standing at the window and jabbering away, about Clara probably, but no one could say for the window was shut. It wasn't bad, you know, only I was glad I had cheated her girlish eyes of the confession they were begging.

On the first Nazi anniversary, two barns on the Hindenburg mountain caught fire. The flames flickered across the snow-covered slopes, melting the ski tracks. The firebug is at it again—they said. They recalled the harvest fires in Reinerz when two sawmills went up in flames and Glonski bought the saws for a song and even hired four of their best workers. Now there were rumours that he was out to get more workers by burning down whatever he could. But Glonski was ready for them. When they came up the drive in their sleighs, stopping at the machine shed and calling for him, he simply picked up the telephone, and in a calm voice asked father to bring the truck. He did not explain, he just stood waiting at the gate. This is your lot, mister, someone said. You've had it now, and high time, too.

They left their sleighs and closed in on him, one of them with a club at the ready. Glonski must have said something because they stopped dead in their tracks. He was leaning immobile against the gate; the machines had been switched off. Once again he spoke softly and they did not move. Then round the corner swung the truck. Glonski smiled, I could see him clearly as he stood waiting for Father to join him. I sometimes think it was at that moment that I began to hate him. He had not miscalculated, he was no longer the thirteen-year-old boy gasping for air with his face covered in cow dung. Now he was sure of himself; never again would he have to drag himself up before them and wipe the muck from his face, hand thrust into mouth to stifle the tears. He had been right in everything since that day, now it was enough to have Father beside him, Father who was protected by his reputation, by his shop, by Anne's going to church every Sunday and by his being the local teacher's father. As I stood there at the hut window, I knew why he had married me and also why he would always be a stranger. But did I tell you that it was a clear frosty day, a crystal day when every moment was brittle? The man with the club stood in front of the group. Father said something. A bit of snow came loose but everything else was still, like a pane of glass that a sudden stone would have shattered. Glonski had not moved; a horse stamped.

Well, it's true no one has actually seen the bastard doing it, said the man with the club.

That was all, just the man's voice and the frost. In those November days it lay heavy on the ground; only at noon did the sun manage to melt the gutters at the edges of the road. The ski-marked slopes, too, darkened at midday. You can imagine the scene and the sound-filled silence of clear frosty nights. The Nazis were at it again; occasionally one of us would listen to the radio. The tourists left early that year, but even they could not entirely escape the frost of those bright nights. Huddled in the Breslau-Berlin express or in the night train to Leipzig or Cologne they passed a station, and a snow-covered nameplate. As they peeled an orange and gazed idly out of the window, they could see wooden trucks covered in hoarfrost. My God—did you see that? They are naked in there! Down with the blinds and the train moves off. Remember?

At night the little stove would go out, and we would wake and shiver. The sun had barely risen across the slope and begun to fall on the window of the blockhut before it disappeared again. From the bed I could see the shape of a man through the pallor of the frozen glass. He must have pressed the palm of his bare hand against the glass, for in the middle of the pane the ice began slowly to recede. Now his mouth was on the pane, his breath widening the hole. His lips kept repeating the same words. I could hear nothing but the noise of the machines that had just started up. Their monotonous roar was muffled by the wooden floor beneath me. So I stood freezing in my nightdress for I had understood Kolczynski's

46

meaning the first time. He, too, realized it and went away. His sleigh, from which he should have been scattering sand, stood in front of the machine shed. For a moment the machines seemed to stop, leaving only the illusory sounds of the frost in the sunlight. Then they began again, drowning the silence of the frost.

In her room on the first floor, Anne was probably unaware of the frost nor could she have heard the crunch of boots a few hours before Kolczynski's hand melted the ice on my window. Later that morning she went to look for Father, Glonski's saviour, and found him just by the Weitspritz sluice. An alder, most of its branches bare of snow and, yes, the sun was shining, you know the rest.

Glonski did not come out with it there and then; that is why I stayed on. Of course, you say, I should have left. Two days later he stepped into the room and turned his back on me, while he warmed his hands. Then he turned—So that is the kind of blood you have, is it?—But even if I had left, where could I have gone? To become a schoolmarm again, lodging with a widow, amongst the furniture of the dear departed? Sustained by the occasional visit of a fellow teacher who drinks nothing but fruit juice? Or live with relatives and become an eavesdropper on life? I simply couldn't have done it. Belief in myself was dwindling and yet, whenever I looked in the mirror, I saw the old Clara, the one in the window behind the rhododendrons. Clara of the dark dress, the teacher with the carefully parted hair, facing a class of wooden-faced children, hateful because they were not her own. Clara, whom I avoided in the mirror, who made me lose weight, change my hair-style, run out and rub my face with snow until it burned as if from greedy kisses or the bites of his ferret teeth. Yes, I lusted for them as for a blade to cut up the face of the old Clara, and how I hated him for it, not because I was a Jewess, but with a flowering hatred of my own.

[Uncle Pomsig had carefully lit a cheroot. The china lamp in front of him split the tobacco smoke into two, sucking it in at the base and releasing it again, milk-coloured, from the top of the shade.]

My hate fed on the thought that it was Father's reputation that had saved Glonski from their vengeance. But all Glonski wanted was a brood mare to sire a son with. A pure creature, neither Jew nor Pole, whose son would never have his face wiped in cow dung. For a time I was that mare. In those frosty days at the beginning of the year I tried to carry on as usual, cooking his meals of dumplings and red cabbage. Huddled before the stove in my dressing gown, I thought it not so bad. Then came the thaw; it was April '34. Once again the waggons bearing the green logs lurched through the mire of the yard. On the northern slopes, dark gullies appeared where the ski-runs had been. In one of them Father's truck stuck fast. Glonski got out: without his windcheater. He was again the grand Glonski with the BMW and the rug over his knees whom I had loved the summer before—from the window behind the rhododendron bush. He went round the truck, lifted the French woman from the seat, and carried her inside to me. For a while it seemed as if the rhododendrons had never existed, that heady summer when we abandoned our dark dresses and the bush gave off its stifling scent. Even so, I stayed on, and when I finally did go and stand before a class again in Breslau, the humiliation was even greater. I would twist the ring I wore on a string round my neck and rub the white band on my finger until it bled. Always waiting until the other woman, too, would be thrown out to share my loneliness.

No, actually I left that same evening. But it's true that I went to Breslau. I wasn't allowed to teach, though, and so I went to work in a grocer's shop, instead. I bided my time, just waiting for it to happen.

So there I was counting the days. True, I did write to her saying that he would sleep with her and then abandon her for bearing the kind of son who might end up having his face rubbed in cow dung. But apart from those letters I let things be and worked quietly in Widow Scholtze's grocery shop. Over my bed was a picture of a lieutenant, next to it a watch with the inscription: Happiness is oblivious of time. Five years they had been engaged, one year of marriage, and then a grenade splinter ended it all in 1918. It was on the Western Front, Frau Schultze said, in France. And now France was in the news again. We kept listening to the special bulletins. I said nothing but I knew perfectly well what must be happening to the Frenchwoman. Now, Glonski's son was no longer safe. The ill-gotten sawmills would never be passed on to him. We heard it all on the German radio. One day her son might be chased across the playground and have his French face driven into the dung, gasping for breath and then retching. . . .

Perhaps he had met her in Breslau, a desirable face reflected in the window of a leatherware shop or a jeweller's. But now the radio blared out against her kind as well. Glonski wasted no time in sending his new wife and son into a camp. Later I met her in the street in Breslau and followed her for a while.

50

She reminded me of Anne. Not the Anne who found her husband dead at the Weisstritz sluice in those hard, frosty November days, and lost her mind, but the woman who used to sit dreamily at the window, caught up in her hopes and desires. The French-woman was a dreamer too; that's probably why I liked her. For apart from that one season of warmth and perfume, I have always kept my eyes wide open. The bitter waking of denial that has its dreams in hatred—who wrote that, I wonder? She never even woke up when she finally got out of the camp where Glonski had sent her. Yet she kept the boy clean and even managed to spoil him, as I discovered later, after her death in the railway wagon. Death itself could only embellish the beauty of the cool tender-ness on her face.

It started with a child's voice from the train in Breslau station. After a pause the voice continued and began singing the first few bars of *Deutschland über alles* over and over again. The steps and curses of the soldiers outside grew louder until the man next to me, the one with the handlebar moustache, went for the boy. Another line rang out before Handlebars reached the door. Grabbing the boy, he thrust his head between the suitcases and hissed—Do you want to get us all locked up with your filthy song? But the train had already begun to move. The wind snatched at the creaking door of the guard's van. The wheels resounded across the points in the fresh October air. Soon be snow, someone muttered. At first I did not recognize her. She lay on her suitcases with a blanket drawn up to her small uptilted face. A bright spot against the dark wall of the wagon. Handlebars still held the boy and only released him when we had crossed the last points. One more squeak, you little bastard, and it's out of the door you'll go. But he gave a laugh as the boy slipped out from under his arm and pressed his face against the tiny pane. He began to count. Light and shadow flickered across his face while trees and bushes sped past. A passing train spattered a staccato of day and night on him. Remaining at the window he would occasionally jerk his head abruptly to catch an escaping wagon. At forty, he would begin all over again in that slight French accent which I had noticed during his singing of the German anthem. It sounded so incongruous among all those gravelly voices, rasping like stones in a mountain stream.

Karl August and his family were done in, as well.

So was Runge.

And so was the one down the road, the one who would never clear his own snow. They didn't spare

52

a single Werewolf alive up there in the mountains—
said Handlebars with a gesture towards the roof.
Yes, his accent stood out like a sore thumb amongst
their guttural drawls. And then I knew for certain.
Glonski's son—I remembered him from the few
times I had seen him in Breslau with the Frenchwoman. Here he was, pressing himself against the
doorway. Our only link with the changing pattern
of the landscape; the trees and the slopes outside. I
watched him incessantly. A small boyish face with an
upturned nose, and so near that I could have touched
him. True his ears stuck out but that was due to his
crewcut. The eyes were quick and bright; not missing
a single train. With that unusually thin mouth he
could have been twenty-three not six. Suddenly I
knew what I had missed in life. It was like looking at
a painting or photograph of a landscape one will
never visit. Well, I loved him now—that's what you
wanted to hear isn't it?—Loved him because he
could have been mine; because I had been cheated
out of him. Whenever I look at that snap behind you;
yes, look at it, it reminds me of a little wooden figure.
Carved in haste but with only a tiny flaw, a tiny
blemish and for that he was rejected. Glonski had
swept him from the table soon after birth like a faulty
carving; and now someone had to bend down to

pick up the pieces. Yes, I could have stretched out
and touched him quietly in that packed, stinking
goods wagon. The Frenchwoman lay peacefully
beneath her cover. So still was she and taking up so
little room that no one would have noticed if she had
suddenly disappeared. Her graceful face lay faint
against the back of the wagon, while the boy's reflected the chequered passage of the journey on his
face. Light and shadow, passing trains and trees and
houses that he alone could see. Someone gave her
coffee, cradling her head as she drank and then
turned her head away. They talked of Görlitz. Just
past it was a delousing station and in the evening the
sanitary corps would come. The voices grew excited
around me:
And I was still thinking I hope to Christ they don't
come in, when there they are and, would you believe
it, under his bed they found ten pairs of shoes from
the Refugee fund.
—Just look at the potatoes.
—It's only Liegnitz.
—Hope to Christ they don't come in.
—He was still wearing his party badge. The Poles
spotted it at once.
—Just take a gander at those potatoes. . . .
The names rushed by again, Breslau, then Walden-

burg. The little woman next to me continued her husband's story about the shoes. As the train settled down to an even speed the voices became clearer again. What's the good of it all, I thought, as he sat again at the doorway, I'll never have him or anyone else either. I've been cheated out of my son. In the evening the sanitary corps will be watching for us. And though he's so close, I might as well be miles away from him. The voices kept up their ebb and flow. Near Görlitz one said, you can catch a connection to Cottbus, and from there to Warsaw, and perhaps even to Brest-Litovsk and to Kiev. Again the voices swelled. Wait, please listen a moment, I can see you are an old party man, what's all this nonsense about a connection at Görlitz. Oh, I see, you are a railway worker. Why didn't you say so in the first place.

The Frenchwoman did not move. In the evening she still lay under her blanket. She had not foraged for potatoes like all the others when the train had stopped near the fields, nor had she used the tin at the doorway. Now in the growing darkness her face became a vanishing speck of mould.

—They're bound to get on at Görlitz.

It's nearly time.

But the rhythm of the wheels never changed, as we passed Görlitz and then a whole string of villages.

We only noticed she was dead when someone tried to give her coffee again. She had not screamed and a soft moan would have been drowned by the noise of the train. So no one had heard it, just the clanking of the wheels—nothing else.

You will probably have to defend him, you know. Though I pray it won't come to that. But if I know him at all, I know he can't be stopped now. That's why I sent you that letter. What was I to say to him, now that he is twenty-three and knows part of the story anyway? You are listening, aren't you?

Anyway, I took care of him in that train. Then came the delousing station soon after Görlitz. They led us all, men and women, into the shower room. All of us stood under the water except for the boy, who watched us defiantly from the wall. There was nothing we could do about it. Everyone told him to look the other way, but he just stood there looking like a child about to be thrashed. Then, with a howl he ran to me, beating his head against my body and shaking me. The others laughed; they hadn't even noticed him before the Frenchwoman died. For one or two days he sat close to me on the floorboards, vomiting once or twice into the tin. But then he returned to his hatchway. In any case he stopped crying.

For the rest of that fourteen days' journey I had eyes

56

only for him. The smell from the tin increased daily as the rattle of the wheels and the grating voices droned on. The names of towns floated by like bloated corpses. And the boy was near me all the time, and I kept sticking the soda-water bottle into his mouth, tilting it so he could suck in the sugared water. Lemonade, he began to call it.

No, it wasn't because of Glonski or the French-woman, it was just that I had never had a child of my own. I never even dared to hope that it could remain like this until I spotted the linen bag he wore around his neck. The papers inside could be lost and the authorities had more important things to worry about at a time like this. After two weeks among their coarse gravelly voices we were unloaded at Gindenhall and—do you remember?—that's when I first came to see you with the boy. [He was pluck-ing at your juniper, and I thought I'd better pretend I was cross and smacked his fingers.] I told you his name was Junk, and that his father had fallen in Moldavia. You swallowed it all, and it was then, perhaps, that I began to despise you. No, it wasn't you really, it was all those who could never change whom I really despised, with their wailing about poor Silesia, and the good old days. What does it matter, anyway? His linen bag contained a card with his photograph, name and the names of his parents. It also had the address of the sawmill and of what I supposed was the Frenchwoman's furnished room in Breslau, after she left the camp. The cardboard looked as if the boy had been having a good chew at it, and the photograph had come loose. It's the one you can see hanging behind you. In the morning when I tried to wash him and he jerked away from the facecloth, all that was left was a thin strip of cardboard and a piece of linen bearing the letters P . . i . . p . . N . . in black print. They stood for Philip Norbert. He must have been trying to destroy his past as he lay at night in the cold of the train. Perhaps it was simply boredom that started him chewing, who can tell? Anyway, the past was gone, his barely remembered father and his French mother whose names he had worn round his neck. All he was left with was her accent—it took me quite some time to rid him of that. But that morning all I did was to make him into my son, forming the new name, Pnip, from the four letters left on the cardboard. So completely did I alter Glonski's cast-off carving that even as he was pulling at your juniper he could barely remember his real name.

For some time Uncle Pomsig had been staring out of the window. In the twilight he could still recognize the top of the picket fence. Above it spread the two wings of a bird in flight. They hovered in the air for a moment then folded back into the bird's body as it alighted. Did she delay in helping the Frenchwoman or did she stop the others from helping her? All that business about the sawmill seemed genuine enough, but what about the linen bag? Pomsig looked for the pigeon again, but it had gone. No, there it was on another fence, head under its wing, probably looking for fleas; now it was still again. Or was it a different pigeon altogether? Then he turned back towards Clara and examined her as one does a china doll. Turning it round and round before returning it to its place.

Just a small point—he said, turning the linen strip over in his hand—couldn't scissors have done this?

Her gravelly voice had stopped. Clara looked out over the redcurrant bushes to the fence and the band of twilight above it.

Suppose you had done it with nail scissors and not he with his teeth, as you claim? But Clara was off again, stones rattling on tin, as if she had not heard his question or did not consider it worth answering.

So she was lying, or telling a half-truth. She must have skimmed over the death of the Frenchwoman. People do not die like flowers, even cut glass can be heard cracking. But what clinched it for Uncle was the boy's green linen bag. Here the story did not hinge on a load of sentimental stuff about trees and flowers and balmy winds; she had made the mistake of preserving the evidence. She must have done it with a small pair of scissors, my uncle claimed, nothing as big as a pocket knife, or a serrated kitchen knife could have made that chain of sickle cuts. Scissors too weak and small to cut the linen in one go. She must have applied the scissors time and again until the cuts looked as if they were made by a small boy, chewing his past away by night. Uncle Pomsig wanted to ask her to show him the scissors from her sewing basket. But the stale air in the room had tired him; in any case Clara continued unchallenged and he remained bent forward across the table—no longer watching her but tracing the fading pattern of the wax cloth, and imagining what really happened on the train when Clara forced the bottle into the boy's mouth. The boy had probably jerked away from her grasp, a schoolteacher's grasp. She had never had children nor had she wanted them except as a weapon against Glonski. But Uncle said nothing about all this, he had ceased for a minute to be interested in truth and falsehood. Instead he just watched Clara's ageless face with its girlish mouth.

He seemed transfixed by it and by the eyes flickering behind her steel-rimmed glasses. He held it all in the palm of his hand. Yet he did not say what he probably ought to have said: I don't believe a single word of it.

IN AN album Clara kept a photograph of the boy in front of a cathedral; dressed up like a little monkey she said. She had found it in Pnip's rucksack together with other photographs of the Frenchwoman, of Glonski, the sawmill and the converted blockhut. In some of the snaps he was two years old, in others a baby of three months sprawling on a bearskin rug. There were group photos, too, Pnip in the Frenchwoman's arms, Pnip on the grass, Pnip on her shoulders. Glonski was present in all of them: but always as if his presence was merely an afterthought. One showed the Frenchwoman at the wheel of the truck. It must have been soon after her confinement. In spite of the swollen face and the shadow-ringed eyes, Clara had to admit that the woman was beautiful.

One of the photographs, which Clara never showed to Pnip, was one of him at the age of five. A stormy sky formed the backcloth to what was probably a crumbling tower of Breslau Cathedral. In the foreground were two plump pigeons, sweeping across the Cathedral front. They must have flown up from a crevice just as the shutter clicked. Above padded shoulders the boy wore a knitted cap on a tiny head, tilted forward. He had a serious face but perhaps there was a hint of a smile. One arm was neatly folded across his chest. The legs ended in black patent shoes. When Uncle Pomsig looked at the little figure in the photograph, he felt that a gust of wind or even the wingbeats of the pigeons could have bowled the boy over.

A year later he would pluck the juniper bush outside Uncle's verandah and have his fingers smacked.

Then came the river, Weinrich and Magosch, and that business with the sandals. Everything about him a bit puppetlike and mechanical; until his smile suddenly changed. Erna. Sunday, and away from school, belting through the autumn mist on his blue bicycle. As he passed clearing after clearing the wind would seize him, taking his breath away and trying to push him back. Then up the last hill before Moslau, balancing on the pedals, his small backside wriggling

63

in the fog. Yes, Erna helped to change him a great deal that autumn. It was because of her that he threw himself across Weinrich the summer before. And though he avoided her all through the winter, next autumn, when Weinrich was training as a teacher and Magosch was a soldier, he began to pay regular visits to Moslau on Sundays. Wriggling up the incline, then down into the valley. Those two would have noticed quite a change in him since their departure. His face bore the rash of pimples that theirs hadn't had for years. Not that Erna was getting all she wanted either. That was just the trouble. Her young body was all promise with its awakening lips, breasts and belly. Even her eyes sparkled with knowing art-fulness. Frau Blume had to keep reassuring her hus-band whilst he watched them walking off together down the village street. A ponytail of brown hair bobbing over a long, cautious face, bubbling with secret laughter. For her Pomeranian drawl forced her for a long time to keep her mouth shut. When she walked, high-slung hips wiggled above a narrow pelvis. On one of those walks between Kuhle's meadow and the copper birches on the hill, some-thing happened to Pnip that Weinrich and Magosch would never have understood. For instance Pnip would have given quite a different answer had he been asked again to take a course at the interpreters' school, now that the Common Market was coming, and languages were the thing. That's what they told him, anyway, in the bright office, from which you could see the tower of St. Blasius and the jumbled roofs of the old town. The tower was being repaired and a basket rose gently up the façade, hung motionless for a moment in the pale blue air and was then pulled in. That's when Pnip had said no to them. Now it all felt different, here in Kuhle's meadow, beneath the birches, with a spotty face and moist palms on a cool day. Erna's little pecks, then the longer kisses ending with bitterness like the stones of sweet fruit. Young breasts nailed against her pullover. Perhaps it was just nostalgia that made Uncle Pomsig blame everything on that. In any case, Pnip was no longer the boy who had been crouching with Pierke, impassively watching the American truck parked among the trees, with a Negro squatting near the open door. Big Negro laughter and hands like palm leaves. It was an old Chevrolet, we all knew about Yankee trucks in those days. Again the laugh, two pairs of legs and the strong, sweating back of the Negro. A cry of lust or rage as they coupled. The Negro sweating and clawing at the grass verge. Behind, the cool faces of two boys aged twelve or

65

thirteen, crouching among the poplars. Pnip only grimaced because of the sun in his eyes. Catapult at the ready he set off through the allotments, as Pierke began to vomit.

No, he was impassive no longer. Now he crushed a sprig of juniper into Erna's neck. The smell of iron and kitchen spices tickled his nose as they lay together in the grass. On the way back he occasionally released a handlebar and smelled his hand for the perfume from her neck. On Sundays he smelt it again as he perfumed her bosom amid whispered promises. That's how it went on for weeks. Then Pnip began to curse himself for what he did to her at night in his thoughts. It would begin as he returned along the asphalt road and continue until he sat with Clara warming himself at the iron stove. At night it was worst in spite of all his efforts, as the acrid stench of the toilet drifted under his blanket.

You might, of course, say that something was obviously wrong with him. But wait until you hear about the calendars. They were the kind firms send out every Christmas. Clara showed them to my uncle. Every day Pnip had been to Moslau was marked. Some dates had a small sign, perhaps a hill or a tree —the purple calendar of '60 was full of oaks and birds. And these calendars were all Uncle Pomsig had to find out what Pnip might be planning to do, and how to prevent him. The more he thumbed through them the more the boy seemed to dissolve into a disjointed string of objects: the remains of a linen bag, a soda bottle, a blue bicycle, a pair of black socks and yogi sandals. Could these, as Clara claimed, solve a crime that lay in the future and for which he might have to provide a defence? He picked up the leaf-green calendar for '61. January—Pnip probably fetched the bicycle from the shed and scraped the ice from the saddle with his knife. Perhaps he stuffed newspaper into his pants before swinging off down the icy track. A copy of the *Frankfurter Allgemeine Zeitung*, maybe, or *Die Welt* or *Der Rheinische Merkur*. Or else the *Gindenhaller Kurier* or the *Göttinger Tageblatt* which Clara watched for news of additions to neighbouring sawmills. At the first hill he had to get off, pushing back his peaked cap and loosening his scarf, perhaps picking at one of the pimples on his once clear forehead. At first he managed to mask the pimples with his hand, but as the cranberry rash spread all over his face he had to lower his eyes before passers by. My uncle skipped the carnation signs for January, only noting an entry about the new tiles on the tower of St. Blasius. You could imagine Pnip making his secret entries, head bent in front of a Martini bottle with its freshly picked white carnation. Practically every page had been filled. But it was in the scarlet calendar that Uncle Pomsig found something that really caught his attention. The stray bitch had crawled into the cycle shed at night and dropped four puppies. Pnip was there first and took one away in his coat pocket. He was already on his bicycle when Clara discovered the others. Holding them like rags or used tea bags she carried them at arms' length to the rainwater butt, plunged them into the water and held them there.

Quickly up the hill and down again went Pnip, his clanging bell bringing Erna first to the window then to the door.

The mother is white with black spots, she crawled into our shed ready to pop, yesterday. Clara drowned the rest in the water barrel. She hates anything like that. This is the only one left: I want you to have it. Me?

Then she was off into the house, calling for her mother. She had begun to show traces of that bitterness about which Otto Blume began to complain that summer.

In the kitchen she laughed. Frau Blume said—what a miserable little specimen, can't you wait for your own? But Pnip was already off, back to the garden shed.

Clara would not talk about it. She evaded my uncle's questions, so the story might have happened quite differently. Look at it this way. Perhaps it was Clara who found the litter. Who kicked the bitch aside and marched with the four of them at arm's length past where the boy stood. Elbowing the cover of the rain-butt aside, she made to thrust the chequered bundle inside. Suddenly Pnip gripped her arm and without a word pushed the cover back again.

Give me one: you can do what you like with the rest. No.

He fought with her then; all trace of the well-known smile had gone. More surprised than angry, she gave in.

All right, you can have one but I don't want this bitch and her rubbish around here. Producing one after the other in my clean straw. Clear off with it then. And she plunged the other three into the water as if she were shoving a lemonade bottle into a small boy's mouth. With the unreasoning bitterness of a childless woman, one who has given up hope, who was left with nothing but a feeling of righteousness, greater even than the need to save life. This was the other side of the coin.

Perhaps there was yet another version of the story. But Clara kept her mouth shut. All this talk of dogs brings me back to the episode with the cat. That had more than one side to it, too. They were all lying in the grass by the Este, the sunlight pressing against their eyelids; their skin tensed by the heat crying out for more water. But they were tired and just wanted to lie in the grass. It was Hans Weinrich who first noticed the cat. Magosch, or was it Schrader, drugged by the sun and water, squashed a horsefly on his knee with a curse. All was silent again. Then the cat reappeared and circled. Weinrich said that they really needed a white one to show up in the water.

Anyway where do we get one and how could we tie it up?

What about a clothes line?

Or a wire.

Whose cat do you suggest?

The Misslings have a white one.

No, Misslings' is black and white.

Doesn't matter as long as it's mostly white.

Once again they flopped back into the grass, blinking sleepily. Pnip was silent the whole time. He lay at the edge of the group watching the Este lap softly against the quay. Next day he arrived with a shopping bag and a clothes line. Hans Weinrich suggested throwing the trussed-up cat into the water and drawing it across the river like a fish basket. The one who threw the cat furthest and brought it back alive, would be the winner. Pnip tied the line round Missling's cat and after letting it run out only two yards asked Hans to tie the other end round his body. At first Hans pretended not to understand, and then he funked it, afraid of getting scratched. That's how Magosch came to be the first. He had the cat tied to him with just enough slack in the line. Then he clambered off the slippery stones and began to swim cautiously. But after only a few strokes, he jerked frantically at the line and tore it loose. By then the cat had torn both his thighs open. Schrader who went next tried it backstroke. The cat allowed itself to be fended off against the current for a while. Then suddenly it was at his shoulders. A scream from the bank made him look up. The claws ripped again and again across his chest. He climbed out, and as he sat staunching the flow of blood with a towel, he looked challengingly at Pnip. Pnip had barely pushed off from the quay when the cat drifted up to him. Just before it reached him, he turned across the current and allowed the cat to drift away with the Este. Now he ploughed diagonally across the current to-

71

wards the opposite quay. At regular intervals he would push the cat away whilst the others watched disappointedly from the shore. Still wiping the red ooze away, Schrader was praying for the wet claws to reach Pnip and open up his face and legs. Weinrich and Magosch were hoping for it too. But though he let the cat come quite close to him, he always managed to evade it. From the bank they saw the sun's rays dipping into the water. The dark sheen of the cat's fur appeared so close to the swimmer at times, that it seemed inevitable. Ever closer came those raking claws but Pnip kept pulling away at the last moment. His waxen face turned skywards seemed to drift apart from the body. Occasionally it dipped beneath the wavelets but reappeared unharmed. It was more like a shell or a wood shaving than the face of a swimmer. While they all leant expectantly forward, Pnip felt the bundle of fur get heavier. Just before he climbed out of the water, he released the line without a single glance behind. Then he lay gasping on the grass and allowed Hans Weinrich to examine him. But there was nothing: the only damage was to Magosch and Rolf Schrader. Although they claimed to have taken the worst out of the cat, they never again called him Pnipsqueak. But then they wouldn't ask him to come swimming with them either. So perhaps the cat had won over Pnip, after all.

But they never realized that there was another side of the story. And though Uncle saw in the scarlet calendar of '62 that Pnip met Magosch the soldier and Weinrich the would-be teacher, that summer, they could not have had much to say to one another. The two of them knew nothing about the puppy and they liked to forget the cat episode. At most, as they walked down the street to the station, past the old houses with St. Blasius beyond [Look, they have replaced the tiles we shot down] they might have realized that Pnip had changed completely.

Look, he's even got spots on his face now!

And we used to say that he'd got damn all in his pants.

Remember in the gym that time when he just stood there watching. . . .

Well, he's changed anyway. Do you remember . . .

What?

That cat. You know, Missling's cat.

Look, they have replaced the tiles.

Almost white it was. Gave old Schrader's chest a good going over. Got a good hiding, too, when he got home for messing the towel up.

We did it with a catapult. Took ages to knock the

first one off. Much simpler with a carbine. . . .
Pnip was the only one to get away with it, remember,
to the other quay and back again?

Was he, said Magosch. But of the stray puppy they
knew nothing. Nor had they seen Pnip's look out
towards St. Blasius and the old city. The basket of
tiles swinging in the blue air as he refused the job.
He regretted it later in Kuhle's meadow but not for
long. His past and all his questions dissolved into
Erna's skin and the spicy, metallic smell of juniper
which he rubbed into her breast. He even forgot the
yogi sandals and the shirt studs.

Frau Blume, too, was satisfied. At least she did not
say anything to Erna afterwards. She was ironing at
the time, occasionally patting her dampened fingers
on the iron and producing a hissing sound. For a long
time they made vague conversation. Frau Blume in
the thick Pomeranian dialect which she had retained
all this time they had been on Franz Kuhle's farm.

Then she began preparing two egg custards and a
seed cake. Imagine her cracked hands greasing the
cake tin and filling it with dough and slices of butter.
She divided the lion's share between Erna and Pnip.
You must remember that they'd all written Otto
Blume off. The Blumes had come from Stettin and
were billeted on the Kuhles in Moslau. Otto had to

74

begin again from scratch, to look for a bed and some chairs; bits and pieces that so quickly become part of us. Then to buy cups to contain the saccharine-sweetened tea from the trading-stamp aluminium teapot. Pots and pans, stoneware saucers, knives and forks with black wooden handles, soup-plates and plates for the vegetables. Then military coats that still showed their camouflage in strong sunlight. On her old Singer, Frau Blume would transform them into skirts and trousers. And Erna needed a satchel and a sledge of her own, for the other children would only give her a ride on Kuhle's meadow on condition that she dragged all their sledges up the hill. Yes, he bought the whole lot. But then he would sit about for days in the kitchen, red-faced, silent and without a shirt. In the mirror frame was wedged an aerial photograph of Stettin, taken from a magazine. It had yellowed with time and the cluster of houses had turned olive green. The sole reminder of those twenty hard years. When Erna used her first piece of Palmolive at the basin he must have felt a twinge of jealousy. In any case, he was furious when she appeared in her first nylons. It was probably because he had not bought them himself, had not even thought of them. She had come to him for her satchel, her sledge and her Palmolive soap; but now she wanted nylons and she got them herself. The mesh against her growing leg drove home to him how times had changed. They were drifting apart. From the table he watched her combing her hair at the mirror; then he said.

Take them off.

Take what off?

Take those damn things off. When you stop flirting I'll buy you a pair myself.

When Blume and the others at last formed an expatriate association it was not out of bitterness. All those who had come to Moslau and Gindenhall had done well for themselves. It was just that they had a belief in a return to the country of their youth, and that they liked to natter about the past. So Blume went around Moslau and over coffee talked about Stettin and a get-together, even mentioning the aerial photograph in his mirror frame. Many attributed his speeches and placards to a yearning for Stettin and the wharves on the Oder. But it was really Erna with her Palmolive and nylons that drove him to start a membership list with monthly contributions. With the newssheets in his briefcase, off he would go every evening around Moslau and on Sundays to Gindenhall, collecting subscriptions. Perhaps he even deceived himself into believing it all. But time was bearing Erna away from him. A new way of laughing, the appearance of a pony-tail in her Madonna-like hair, coincided with the arrival of Pnip. She no longer plaited her hair; she was growing up. Frau Blume would look up from the kitchen table or ironing board and say:

All dressed up and off on his rounds. Believe me, it's getting quite like old times again.

Otto now shaved more carefully and dragged his fading black hair into place before leaving the house. With his stocky frame clad in a checked sports jacket and wearing a tie, he set off, briefcase in hand, down the village street. As she watched from the window above the geraniums, Frau Blume recalled the days of their youth in Stettin. So absorbed was she, that she did not notice the swift entry of Kuhle.

Off to flog his papers, is he? You are a cool one, never a word to him about our little set-to in the stable.

Shut up.

Running around with that briefcase and starting the whole thing over again, just like Hermann says.

Why don't you shut up.

Fixing up meetings in Gindenhall, they are, dragging the kids in too. Got an even bigger flag now; so Hermann tells me—he's always right.

I don't want to know what Hermann has to say.

Had your skirt down quick enough in the stable didn't you? And it wasn't only the milk you were in a hurry for either.

Shut up, you dirty old man. I can hear Erna coming.

It wasn't long before Otto delegated the stamps and newssheets to his wife. She combined their distribution with reminiscences about the old days. About the dances, the sand on the banks of the Oder; about the military parades with Otto marching in front as drum major. She even managed to pass on a few recipes.

And Otto ceased to be the silent watcher. Released like a wound-up spring, he became an orator. He forgot those long years in Kuhle's kitchen and for a time became a hero.

Gindenhall has its cycle races. Even my uncle gave up working in his office that Sunday and listened to the loudspeakers. It was a warm spring morning. The church-bells rang out and handlebars glinted in the sunlight. A bunch of cyclists was coming up the main street. With a whine of wheels and gears they swept past the platform draped with strange flags, up the street to the station and the Este beyond. Then back down the main street, skirting the platform. The sewing machine whirr increased again. My uncle knew that someone had presented a ham for the cause of Silesia. After a long pause, a small camera had been added by someone else and Holtzmann gave a push button radio from his new music shop. Even while the race was still being run, a fourth donor added a refrigerator.

Otto presided over the contest which this year was held in honour of goodness knows what Stettin anniversary. I remember thrusting between the legs of two men who must have towered over me at that time. With my stomach against their thighs I caught a glimpse of the man at the microphone holding a ham. As he distributed the prizes he added a few words suited to this auspicious occasion. There was particular gratitude for Holtzmann's gift, or so my uncle told me. The man ended with a call to Prussia and Upper and Lower Silesia to rejoin the Fatherland. All depended on the youth, the gallant German youth. But their elders, and particularly those from the East must also not be forgotten. No doubt, he said all the right things.

Works for an insurance company, does he? one of the bystanders said. How old is he do you think? He's got a future, that one. Let him go into politics and he'll have my vote.

Brilliant idea that, just the flags and nothing else at all.

But all I could hear at the time was the loudspeakers and the sound of the racing bikes. Still, from what Uncle Pomsig told me, I imagine that it was a different Otto who returned to that kitchen in Moslau. He may have been a little condescending when Frau Blume helped him out of his suit and sweaty shirt. Ordering his beer he sat down next to his daughter, who slyly asked him the obvious questions. He told of the cycle race and the old days as drum major in Stettin. The nylons were forgotten. They sat drinking the Dortmund beer until they both noticed with roars of laughter that she was drunk for the first time. Lore Wellschert was a great one for glue, as we all realized when her hand-made posters began to appear. One on a hoarding outside the school, another across the window of the sweet shop, and then a whole rash of them on the wall where the platform had stood the day before. A crowd gathered round them to read of the black deeds of Otto Blume in Stettin. Old Magosch was saying: It's that Lore Wellschert, pay no attention. She's barmy. I saw her with those placards and a pot of glue. Where are you off to, said I, but she didn't say a word. Then I went into Giorgio's. Cleaning his ice trays, he was, when he let out a terrible curse and went tearing outside. Too late, she had slapped the bloody thing right across his window and was tearing down the street. Off I went after her. Slapping them everywhere, she was, even on car windows.

Yes, it was first-class glue. As we stood watching, two constables tried to scrape it away but two weeks later the black and white paper was still there. It was Lore who sowed the seed that finally drove Erna to seek marriage as an escape from Otto Blume's red-faced silence.

Now, the early sun hung over the geraniums again as they burst into bloom. Swarms of sparrows and pigeons whirled overhead, their wing beats turning into muffled claps at the tolling of the Moslau bell. It was Sunday and Erna stood at the window, much as Clara used to do. She leant against the glass, spelling out a word with her finger, and waiting for the sound of a cycle bell. When it was nearly time, Frau Blume would raise a teasing eyebrow. In that last summer, which Uncle was following in the scarlet calendar of '62, Erna no longer demanded chastity on their long walks. She had combined her mother's teasing ways with the obstinacy of her father and the kisses became more passionate. That summer the geranium scent lay thick in the air. In the afternoons

81

they sprawled by the sea close to the autobahn.
Scooters droned past on the roadway. Words falling
like droplets. His hand sliding up her nylons.

No.

It's only as far as your knee.

By mid-summer he could reach the village in the
time it took to smoke a cigarette, compressing those
geranium days tight together, and rushing headlong
towards autumn. The new experience of speed gave
Pnip something that the yogi sandals, the shirt studs
and Missling's black and white cat had never done.
Yes, his scooter gave him an edge over Weinrich and
Magosch and, who knows, it might even help him to
conquer Erna.

Climb up.

I'd rather walk.

But he dragged her on to the pillion. The rush of air
made her cling tight to him, and as the machine
slithered to a halt, they tumbled off into the grass
together. Again the heady smell of vegetation.
Summer itself seemed determined to overcome her;
cutting into her flesh like a giant rasp. Stop it, she
would say: but did not mean it. Waiting for his hand
with that biting juniper smell to try again.

[Blume would follow her with his eyes in his shaving
mirror when she came home. Palmolive would hide

the smell of the juniper. As tea was poured, she would stand squeezing her stockings in a towel, carefully avoiding the washing-up water and Otto's shaving lather. Or glancing at the aerial photograph of Stettin in the mirror frame, at the photograph that told her nothing about what it had really been like there, playing with dolls or later using your ring to carve names and dates on a window pane.] Pnip, drugged by the juniper, would thrust himself desperately against her but she would turn away from him and gaze at the birch trees, motionless above the sharp, prickling grass. All around was the smell and burnt straw and juniper.

Shall we go, he asked her after a while.

Yes, let's, she said, you go on ahead.

The geraniums were in full bloom below Kuhle's kitchen window that year and chattering sparrows swarmed around the onion bed, before a gust of wind dispersed them. Frau Blume would bend patiently over the sink, where Franz Kuhle would often surprise her.

What do you want?

He would stand in the doorway, watching her bent back and sturdy legs. Then he might talk about the dog. Because she had been good to him he had given it milk when it was still a puppy. But now it was becoming a nuisance on the farm and he had to keep driving it off with a dung fork or a bucket yoke. Look, you must get rid of this mongrel. It's enough that we have to put up with you, let alone that filthy brute.

What is it you really want?

From Stettin, eh?

Come on out with it.

Stettin, he repeated, then—has Erna ever been . . . She did not move from the sink and kept her hands immersed in the soapy water.

You filthy old swine, she said.

His clothes stank of sweat. A mop of red hair towering over a dank shirt. Then he would speak again from the door:

Get rid of that mongrel.

One day Erna stood in the doorway. He swung towards her and Frau Blume screamed. Erna stumbled back and ran off, her feet hammering along the passage.

The fat red geraniums were still in bloom, just as they were on that day when Erna ran away from Franz Kuhle. But the small window panes no longer reflected the sun's copper glow. They showed a spot of misty white, and behind them lay that scent of decay that kept driving Pnip to Moslau.

84

That filthy dog again, Franz Kuhle complained.

Yes, I know—said Frau Blume standing a little wearily in the kitchen. Pnip and Erna led the dog away. Franz Kuhle's red mop of hair followed them past the window, past the geraniums with their odour of rotting foliage. The dull sheen of a zinc bucket, the rose bush, and then he ambled out of view. Pnip struggled to stop the dog from dragging him into the meadow. He stood panting with damp, reddened palms. Erna took the lead and laughed at his clay-spattered trousers where the dog had jumped up at him. Now the dog ran up to the birches, stopped, then dashed off around the trees. Erna was laughing, but not so much at the dog's antics as at Pnip's stupid, incredulous face. And all because of this spotted mongrel, this fragile toy he had once produced from his pocket, which had now run off, after covering him in clay, bounding easily up to the birch clump whilst Pnip struggled breathlessly after it. The dog froze as it saw a crow then made off again along a furrow. Erna loved it, for it was strong and it belonged to her. It was good to see Pnip blushing at last.

Come on, let's run after him.

O.K.

Come on then.

The rim of the sun was now resting on the birches,

so that Erna had to squeeze her eyes as she peered for the dog.

You know, I simply adore him.—She laughed again and turned towards Pnip. Matted sunlight on her hair and then her nylon-clad legs.

Don't look at me like that.

Her hair dissolved.

I'm not a dog, don't look at me like that.

Grasping his hand she began dragging him towards the sun-filled birches. Up the slight incline they ran with the speed of a cascading brook. Now the dog was out of sight. She laughed again; sunlight glancing from her slim body while she raced along. Head flung back as if she were gulping down water.

Now Pnip was running faster. He released her hand and called the dog. Before them the burnished copper of the beech leaves. His tie beat into his face. The wind rose; they leant against it as it thrust into Erna's hair and brushed against her cheeks. The birch on the summit bowed to the side, releasing the sun, then sprang back again. Erna was at the top, Pnip heard her call. Then without stopping she was off, out of sight. Pnip stopped. The birches bent aside again and he felt the wind in his face. Then it was calm, the silence after the run; sweat trickled pleasantly into his mouth. Laughing softly, he wiped his face, and watched the birch with sensuous lassitude. Now he could hear a dog and a cow, then a shout; but he was not really listening. The same aloofness with which he afterwards claimed his lace had come loose. Even though he was wearing black slip-on shoes. Erna had found the dog. She braced herself against the wind, then raced down to get the dog away from Franz Kuhle and his cow. Now the dog leapt at the udder and tumbled aside as Kuhle's boot connected. Raising the pail swiftly above the mongrel's head, Franz brought it down precisely, crushing its skull.

Pnip had reached the birch and was pressed against it. Below him, Erna was hammering against Kuhle's chest. For a time he suffered her as if he were deep in thought. Then suddenly he caught her hair, twisted it round, and flung himself on top of her as she hit the ground—while the boughs rose up into the sun-filtered air, rested, began slowly to drop again, to waver, forcing Pnip time and again to follow their rise and fall with his eyes.

IT WAS the time of the dahlias when Clara suddenly stopped sleeping. She would not even bother to lie down on the straw mattress. Her sleepless eyes watched the invisible ceiling. When Pnip entered at night he no longer heard her turn on the camp bed, calling out of sleep—You are late, supper's in the larder—in her sharp voice. When he lay down now on his bed among the smells of creosote and damp he could see her seated at the window, in her high-necked dress and lace collar, the thinning hair compressed into a bun. Perhaps the headlights of a passing car would suddenly reveal her face, the strange vigour of her mouth and eyes. That's how it was the night after he had left the office for the last time, when the window had showed its copper glow from afar, when he had sat by the Este looking for

Hawe, when he had seen her dim outline behind the window, when he had hesitated, probably without knowing why, although she claimed later that his pause was significant. Only the switching on of the ceiling light had startled her. Switch it off, it's too early—she said and straightened her back. Later she maintained that it was the only thing to do, but no one believed her. He waited a moment then walked out. He drove along the Este past the bank where he had been sitting earlier, then on to the weir. The water lapped, soft and remote across the flat stones. He drove on, down the rattling cobbled streets, as familiar as the lines on his hand, and drifted through the crumbling, decaying labyrinth of houses like a leaf on water.

Hunched in the opposite corner, on a beer crate, Hawe saw him enter. Pnip bent beneath the vaulted ceiling, heard their squeals, and disappeared behind the dancers. Quite suddenly the dance floor emptied except for a single couple. They moved slowly with bent knees and shuffling feet, never raising their eyes from the swivelling hips. The loneliness of bodies copulating apart. Each was the bee and the flower. They moved precisely under their own gaze. The boy would occasionally bend to the ground as before an idol. Before Pnip who stood on the cellar steps. As a fleshy saxophone muffled the beat of drum and guitars and the floor filled again, they drew away, slithering past sweat-stained jeans, duck's arse haircuts and the vacuous smiles you see on women after orgasm. At a table they sank down with eyes only for each other. A wail of saxophones hit the walls.

Let's get out of this hole, I've got five bottles of booze upstairs in the car.

Hawe's smooth face was thrust up to him, a strand of blond hair across the forehead. Come on, let's go. Bent shapes against the roof as they climbed the stairs. Then the dull evening air motionless over the houses of Gindenhall. The music rose up from the cellar, competing with the night-stillness of the town. A quick gulp or two from the water bottle and back into the cellar. Then up the stairs again and into the Fiat. Each in turn pressing the beak of the soft bottle to his lips and swallowing rubber-tainted brandy— Hawe brought it back from Spain every fortnight.

Stop pretending. I know perfectly well that you're looking for her. And all about her and Kuhle, too.

I'm not bothered.

She was here two hours ago.

I'm not bothered, I said.

Turning into a proper little tart. Kuhle knocked her

off—you knew that, didn't you? She was drunk and tired, ended up in Baldie's BMW.

The timber merchant?

No, the one with the sawmills.

I know, the one from Gottsfelde.

Yes, Glonski, comes here for a pick-up sometimes. That's your man.

As Hawe started the car, Pnip thrust the beak of the rubber flask to his mouth and took a long swig of the Spanish brandy. The air stirred itself and tugged at the car as it left the town. Now Hawe took a pull on the flask. In the twilight a village swept into view and was gone. Moslau appeared at the bottom of the hill.

They say there's a do here tonight.

The headlights flickered between the brown-lacquered trees. Then a gate, a curtained window above geranium pots.

The car nodded as it turned back over the corrugations of the square. Slowly the headlights moved across a row of election posters. An old man's head above a younger one with part of the mouth and chin torn off. As they swung on to the autobahn again, Pnip might have thought of the man who built them all. Or of Bismarck and what he had to do with herrings. Of a soda-water bottle and a

91

woman dying unnoticed as he squatted close to the doorway of a railway wagon, counting the carriages of passing trains. Another pull at the brandy.

His name's Glonski, you said.

Yes.

Drive me back.

At the car park, Hawe leant out of the window and jeered at Pnip, who was mounting his scooter.

You're too late—turn back before you get cold feet again like last time.

And all Erna wanted was a break with the past. She was tired of the geraniums, the injured face of Otto Blume, of her mother continually at the sink or chopping onions at the table. But Uncle Pomsig maintained that Erna went to the cellar not for the mischief that Hawe implied, but simply to meet Pnip. Perhaps she wanted to tell him that everything was all right now, that it was all over and almost forgotten, that he should come back to her. Anyway, she sat against the side wall of the cellar peering intently at the descending legs on the stairs. That's why she failed to notice Hawe until he bent over and spoke to her for a moment before the dancers brushed him aside. He tried again, telling her about the booze in his car but did not notice the eyes focused on the stairway or hands tearing nervously at a beer mat.

She dismissed Hawe with a laugh and he glided away, but not before he had noticed her swollen belly. She was wearing the nylons Otto Blume so hated. Her crossed legs slid apart and she left them to the gaze of the new occupant of Hawe's seat. After the interval the music began again. As it spiralled round her, she threw back her head and laughed, revealing her glimmering teeth. But despite her laughter and the music she was like a small animal awaiting slaughter. A good hour lay between this moment and Pnip's arrival in the cellar, and even longer between her departure in the BMW, the driver of which handed Hawe a banknote through the window, and Pnip's starting of his scooter.

Erna, who had more than an hour's start, only noticed the moonlight on the last part of her journey. Then she leant forward from the seat and, with an habitual gesture, pushed a strand of hair across her temple and under the clip on her neck. Pnip, in pursuit, allowed the journey to flow into him. It carried him along, fusing him to the concrete surface. All form and thought were surrendered; only a touch of bitterness remained. A fleeting regret that he could not dissolve in the motion. He passed a road-up sign and braked hard to avoid potholes which the BMW had crossed with ease. Shadowy trees on the slopes flitted by. Beside her, the man was still silent. Erna could see his profile with its narrow mouth. He glanced at her briefly then returned his attention to the road, milk-washed by the moon. Pnip felt a pain in his back from crouching so long over the scooter. He straightened his arms and stood up in the saddle but stiffness and jarring potholes were gaining the upper hand. He swerved out to overtake a cyclist. The buoyant feel of flight had gone. Scattered trees fringed great pools of darkness that grew deeper as the headlight flickered past. Pnip's back was really aching now, the last drowsy comfort of uniform speed gone. So his name is Glonski; but what about Hawe? Why the hell should I turn back? I'll go straight up to them and load her on to the scooter. Probably start crying. But once I'm there, I know I will do it. He crouched low again to speed his journey. Then he slowed down, and the wind ceased to buffet him. He parked the scooter at the kerb, between two lonely lanterns. Here the wood-carts had channelled a path into the entrance, and here Erna had glanced again at her companion, or rather at his profile and his bejewelled fingers on the steering wheel. She had often seen his car parked outside the cellar. As they swung into the drive past the very spot where Pnip was to stop an hour later, the driver loosened his scarf. Two windows in the house were lit, she noticed; then the car sped past the stone steps of the escarpment and passed the lily pond. The moon was half-covered by a poplar tree. Pnip could almost hear the moonlight hammering against its metallic leaves. Now he had passed Vaake and Veckerhagen, the first two villages on the Este. The pain in his back became unbearable and he kept wriggling on his seat. Now the light was on his face as the man turned towards her. Erna saw that it was old and brittle. In spite of the scent of shaving soap it had lost all its sparkle. Partially preserved like the faces of many old doctors or men in theatre bars. Uncle Pomsig would not agree, though he always called Glonski one of the old fish in the sea. He used ointment and tonic water and ultra-violet lamps to stem the ravages of time, but it didn't really help. For there was always, you must remember, the school-yard and the immaculate son who turned out to be just another sham from an impure stable. All this was engraved in his face. The car slowed and skidded along the ramp of an Esso station. Perhaps Erna did not think of him as an old fish but she must have noticed his thin lips and sharp teeth and the assurance with which he got out without telling her to come or to stay inside. Not only did he take her for a whore but for a whore who would do as she was told. Then the quiet confidence with which he climbed in again and threw chocolates and cigarettes into her lap. He kept silent when she said—Won't you please turn round—then started the car and turned into the road—Please, I feel rotten, take me back. Then away from the petrol station and the Esso sign; red letters on the aseptic white background.

Look, I thought it would be all right, but I can't go through with it. I think it's coming. His eyes remained passively on the road as his ruthless hands grasped the steering wheel.

I tried to get rid of it—then I thought it was gone. Anyway I don't go with just anyone. I know Kuhle —Oh Lord, I can feel it coming, it should have been all right until tomorrow.

Erna began to pray. At Gieselwerder, the road surface changed from asphalt to concrete, and Pnip had to slow down. Wooden fences, dung heaps, a pub at the end of the village, then past a barn basking in the moonlight.

I swore to myself I would never sin again if I got rid of it.

Be quiet now—he said as the car turned into the drive—you shall have a room to yourself and tomorrow a woman will come to look after you. It didn't seem to matter when all he did was just stand there under the birches, and watch.

I know, but it's all right now, just be careful how you get out. Don't fill my car full of this muck.

The moon shining diagonally across the barn behind Gieselwerder. Pnip opened the throttle wide. The pain in his back was getting worse all the time.

On the outskirts of the next village he slowed down as he saw a car approach; then he turned round and followed it back. Uncle Pomsig later suggested that, under the first street lamp or lighted window or even the petrol station, Pnip recognized Hawe in the car. Anyway they met again a little later. But why bother talking about supposed street lamps and petrol stations.

Just let's say he did not really know why he turned round. It could have been the moon or the pain in his back. But it was probably a mere chance that caused him to brake and swing round. He could no more have told you why than he could have given his reasons for refusing to go to the interpreters' school or watching mutely from under the birches. The most he could have told you was that the basket had risen up the tower of St. Blasius, or that the birches were moving in the wind, while he felt his

97

silence run over him passively, as water runs over still hands.

Choose what reasons you like. He might even have wanted her to turn into a whore.

Meanwhile she had spent more than an hour in the wooden house with its functionless pillars simulating a country estate. Erna claimed later that he put her in the sitting room off the entrance. Then he bent over and spoke to her, poised for a reply. She was wearing a red knitted jersey and a crumpled skirt. Machinery echoed outside. He said it again, expecting at least a nod. But she remained silent as if he wasn't even there.

Once again in the doorway. The odour of dew-wet plants.

Right, then I'll drive you home.—Off down the drive and into the road. Small steps, but it did not really help. He followed and once again he offered to take her home. She remembered the easy chair and his hand on her back—So we have an agreement, then, Pomsig shall witness it, if you know what that means. If it's a boy you get the money within the year. Amid all her pain she remembered, that, and those eyes watching her from beneath the birches. Erna hurried on.

IN THOSE days Glonski had had the good sense to buy a power saw. My uncle told me all about it. He had gone along more to see the man who had vanished in Bad Reinerz and reappeared in Gottsfelde than out of interest in gear wheels and electric motors. Anyway it was quite an event for someone to buy a power saw in those days. Glonski had it mounted in the refugee camp of all places. It was hard enough for the sawmills even to get customers for firewood. Matties was Glonski's sole worker in his first year of business. Everyone claimed they sawed wood by day and stuck it together again at night, just to look busy. God knows, he was capable even of that. But he lacked the money to buy the site outright from his employee, Matties. Uncle Pomsig claimed he got it by promising to employ its ex-owner in the mill. Some people whispered about werewolves and a Yankee lorry that had a mysterious accident. And Matties told his own story. In any case, Glonski and Matties could be seen sawing away at those supposedly resurrected boards in the late summer of '45. By noon every day their unemployed neighbours would gather at the fence and mock the sweat-stains on Matties's shirt. The whole thing is make-believe, I say; there's not even firewood about. That's what I think too; he's always coming to the kitchen and asking Katie about our barn. Talks about buying the bloody thing, he does. She says You must be mad. By the time I get there, he's trying to lift out the bloody doorpost.

What's the matter with him?

Won't bloody well open his mouth, but before you know where you are he's got the door off. I always say that Matties . . .

Refugee, my arse; he's a bloody red or a madman.

But Glonski sweated on with hardly a glance at them, driving Matties and himself as if every second counted. Like Otto Blume, he probably felt the loss of his former power more than his vanished possessions. Glonski was not resigned to his fate. Rather his disappointment, as Uncle Pomsig admitted, made him fight without scruple for a single objective. This ageing, self-controlled man who had suffered the same fate as Otto Blume, must have taken the loss like a gambler. Now he pursued the same course again with the thrust of a deflected bullet. So when Uncle came to inspect the saw, Glonski was already up to his waist in stagnant water. A nearby river was leaking into the ditch close to the saw. Glonski, Matties, and two other workers were ramming poles into the mud and packing the threatened wall with sods. Then Glonski was hauled up. Ignoring Pomsig, his guest, he wrung the water from his cord trousers and ordered his workers back to the saw. Only when it was whining away again, the afternoon sunlight striking its blade, did he sit down on a beech stump close to my uncle. The noise of the saw seemed like a shout of triumph to him while he rested for a moment. Then he began to talk as he probably did with Matties on those evenings when they drank in the machine shed until one of them slid under the table. He talked about that summer of '45, about Matties's hut, before which they say he appeared with a loaf of bread and a sack of promises.

So you're from Silesia.

What about it?

Nothing, but why come to me?

The next day they began clearing the site behind the hut to build a new shed—the very one whose one wall Glonski preserved against all reason. Soon afterwards Uncle received the first reports from the irate small holders on market days. They whispered about Nazi saboteurs and sand. They would sit wreathed in clouds of smoke from home-grown or smuggled tobacco and tell about Glonski drawing plans of the machine shed in the sand. Instead of measurements he used dates, and every date meant a day of work. Matties had suddenly jumped up, scattering the schedule with his boots. Glonski waited for him to finish then punched him hard in the face and turned away. It was then that Matties had raised the shovel over his head. His wife stood in the doorway of the hut frozen in a silent scream. But all Glonski did was to say something very quietly. He turned away and began pouring out more sand.

O.K.—one claimed he heard Matties say—you win, but Christ knows, it's not fair.

But all this was only rumour. Uncle learned something more tangible about Glonski that cloudy afternoon. They were sitting on the beech logs against the back wall of the old hut. The new saw was still being tested. Glonski began to describe his homeland, and a similar sawmill on the slopes of the Adler mountains. He talked of a village, a house with a single room and of the school in Habelschwerdt. Of Jan Glonski, the Polish farm labourer and his seven or eight children. Now the fitters had switched off the saw as they again adjusted the gearwheels. Glonski could remember little of his brothers and sisters beyond their communal bed, their small bodies clinging together for warmth and their faces hiding under the blankets whenever they heard their father enter, dead drunk. At night the boy would sometimes feel his mother's breath over him. When he finally left home, he missed her and her alone. He was thirteen when he went away to the little sawmill near Reinerz. Then on to Weisstritz, the shrewd purchases of wood, the windcheater, and a girl named Clara Junk from the grocery shop. He had asked for her hand; no, it wasn't like that. He had gone shopping for her in the village, the same way he would buy a lampshade or a stoveplate for his blockhut. Perhaps Clara's story of the gladioli was false, no more than wishful thinking. In any case he knew what he was about. He would not have hesitated as Pnip had done because of a swaying basket or a waving birch. No, Glonski had the clumsy assurance of an armoured car, and needed it, for he always remembered Habelschwerdt and the schoolyard. He had been thirteen at the time and had a syrup sandwich every morning for breakfast. He would eat two more, prepared by his sister, at school in the yard. The bread was so hard that it required a great deal of chewing. But his memories of the school were blurred. Just an occasional fleeting impression of pain. He remembered the bright blue shorts and the haircut his sister gave him. His hair used to hang in a fringe diagonally across his broad forehead above the odd projection of his jaw which lent his pathetic little face the seeds of grimness. Cows were driven across the red clay of the yard twice every day. On that morning, he claimed, they were playing a war game in the cold, violent sunlight. Then they rested, gasping as they munched their sandwiches. Off again they chased, then halted.

There he is again, look at his filthy trousers and his sticky mouth. His old man's a bloody Pole. Come on, let's get him, the dirty Pole.

They all set upon him. Small pinched figures, he described them to my uncle; he recalled the whole scene as if he had been a light-sensitive plate, taking in the smallest detail. They formed a circle round him but he broke away and ran. Red clay bordering the playground. Their feet striking up the gravel as they chased after him, cornering the Pole, hunting him down like hounds in full cry. He ran, in his sky blue linen trousers, across the meadow, veered, and swung away again as one of them tripped him up. The cows were driven across twice every day so they did not have to look far. His face was pressed into the dung until he gasped for air. Then again, right into the middle of it. They stopped, silent except for their panting breaths. The teacher was standing next to them. He was young and chubby with flaxen hair. It was the memory of this teacher's pity, as he came up out of the dung, that was the most painful. The rest could be forgiven.

The saw remained silent. For some time the wind had been freshening, now it bore into the sawdust of the yard and swept it aloft for seconds. They sat on the beech logs as raindrops began to fall, then they went into the engine shed still talking of the thirteen-year-old boy. He had tried to vomit at the river on the way home; later he tried again. He never forgot; his skin had grown thinner that day and his brain had frozen. It was then that he had resolved with all the solemnity of a thirteen-year-old boy, never to come back until he had vanquished the red and white colours of Poland, the syrup sandwiches and the weakness of short trousers. He would run a sawmill, just like the father of the one who was the leader of the pack and had tripped him. And he himself would have a son whom no one would dare touch, of birth so perfect as to command unquestioned obedience and respect. Now the shadows of the birches were creeping swiftly across the square. Water again seeped into the ditch close by the old wall, the one that had been left standing on Glonski's express orders. It now provided an unnecessary disguise for the brick machine shed. Again Glonski tightened his cord trousers and lowered himself into the water. He began obstinately and feverishly to pile up the stones and planks and sods of earth that Matties kept handing down to him. The clouds were now moving more slowly, and the last drops of rain trickled from the trees with the irregular tickings of a cheap watch. Glonski continued to pile up clay against the now useless shed, protecting his own creation. The ridicule was past, all he had to fear now was old age, so that, a few years later when Erna smelled his too-youthful scent, he had precious little time left for signing the contract.

Pnip must have had a suspicion that Glonski was more than just Erna's lover. How else can one explain his sudden about-turn, and his later reappearance at Clara's hut? She could see him from the window, approaching slowly, parting the moon-sprayed bushes. He was probably irritated by the wet branches in his face. Or by the thought of Hawe lying dead drunk in the shed amid the rotting straw bales and potatoes and the smell of vomit and the hot Fiat engine. Pnip overcame his own urge to retch by thinking of fresh jam and a plate of crushed berries sprinkled with milk and sugar; his favourite breakfast, Clara called it. From the window she saw him halt behind a bush and then hurry on. All around moonlight was hammering on the bushes and shadowy dahlia blossoms. The same moonlight that had shone on Erna's hair the night the two of them followed the windings of the aluminium-tinted Este. A fragment of moon had appeared from behind a cloud. It grew, spreading itself like white paint and hung poised above the river. They were both silent as he followed her along the narrow path. Erna's hair was now the colour of mouldy bread. It gleamed invitingly but fiercely from beneath a clip. So they walked on between the needle-like shadows of the grass. Perhaps Pnip wanted to ask her or just lower her tenderly into the grass and bring them both within the protection of their love. Erna walked more slowly now with a grace combining desire and guilt. Finally she stopped. Whenever they left the village on warm afternoons he had pleaded with her.

107

But when the sun had culled the aroma from the juniper bushes in the evenings she had always refused him. Now as they stood here at the river she finally offered herself and he did not know. All he could see was the cold, metallic moon between the porcelain branches. Finally she said: Let's go back. I've got a headache. But all that was way back.

Clara had seen the car outside the shed. She had been watching Pnip for some time. Then she heard his footsteps on the flagstones and the sound of the door opening. They faced each other for the third time that evening. Maybe she lacked the strength now to be afraid, and he saw it. He realized that his question was pointless now even had he still wanted to ask it. All she would have replied in that barren rasp of a voice containing all the bitterness and laboured plans to regain Glonski for herself, was—Yes, it is Glonski, he and the Frenchwoman. And then he would barely have heard her. For what was going round and round in his head until it began to pound was why, in all those years, Glonski never told him, not even once, not one single time—All right, it's me, now shut up —just that, and he would not have bothered him again.

Well?

I thought . . .

Look, I only want to know one thing, why didn't he ever say anything?

You mean Glonski?

Yes, after all he had all the photos and letters you wrote. You were always writing letters to him. If I came back early or woke up you would stuff them into the green folder under the mattress.

Yes, it's true—said Clara, adding in a matter-of-fact tone—but he instructed his lawyer, Pomsig, to burn them all unopened. So he doesn't even know what you look like. Now please leave me.

Once again his shadow passed the window between the dahlias and the currant bushes. Then throwing himself on the wet straw bales next to Hawe he grasped for the rubber bag, clutched the spout with his teeth, and gulped the stuff down until it left him trembling. Hawe was still asleep, his gaping mouth fringed with spittle and dried vomit, like fragments of skin around a gunshot wound. Pnip turned away. Again he could almost hear the moonlight drumming on the roof of the shed, on the top of the car and, with tiny taps, on the clay floor, right to the bales where Hawe lay. His head had slipped from the bales, the mouth was gummed up with vomit. Pnip saw him shake himself and retch again, half-rising, and tried unsuccessfully to shut out the sounds. Why did it have to be this bastard of all people who told me—and the longer he looked at Hawe the more he felt like vomiting himself. He began to beat him slowly and systematically. Hawe's head slid further down on to the clay floor before he regained consciousness. Clinging to Pnip's arm he pulled himself upright. Then they fell together and rolled across the floor to the door. Then Hawe gave up and accepted the regular punches which came between wilder and wilder gasps. At last, Pnip was exhausted and flopped down on a straw bale. Some time later he heard the hissing of the rubber bottle as Hawe, now upright, filled his mouth. Why, oh why, did it have to be him of all people? Somewhere an owl screeched. Pnip did not see the stick crashing down. Again they wrestled on the clay and staggered out onto the grass between the bushes. Now Hawe was beating Pnip's head against the bush. Then Pnip managed to drag Hawe down by his jeans, held his face steady, and hit it hard. Again the owl screeched. Hawe lay still for a while. At last he got up and rinsed his mouth with the Spanish brandy. He held the stuff for a second or two then gulped it down.

Well, at least I know how old I am, Hawe said. He came the spring Matties's wife died, and when I was ready to be christened Matties had to say he was the father. Just as he refused to acknowledge a French half-breed as his son. . . .

Pnip lay motionless on the straw bale, his arms crossed behind his head, and looked out of the shed door.

I don't know why you should bother with Erna. He's having her too. All he wants is bloody brood mares.

The owl flew up and hung a silent shadow in the light before swooping away. Again its cry.

I grant you that the whole thing is merely surmise on my part, and that it could all have happened quite differently, too. The only thing that is certain is the end. That's no longer a question of photos and calendars. We arrived some time after the first siren had sounded and by that time Pnip was crawling through the needled ground of the pine plantation. Between crashes of collapsing beams and timbers he could hear Hawe calling for him. That night the two of them had got up again and gone on to the sawmill. Matties claimed later that he had seen the whole thing outside the machine shed where he was keeping nightwatch. The headlights approached down the Este valley and stopped at the entrance. Then someone in a white shirt came round the house and went in swiftly through the unlocked door. He must have crossed the hallway along which Erna had walked, passing the living room and the sideboard, opening the door to the office, climbing silently up the stairs to the rooms across from the machine shed. In the moonlight, Matties saw the row of windows and in one of them a dark silhouette, a broad fore-head and nose, a slightly drooping mouth and a large chest. It remained for a time then ducked away, and like a fish passing from tank to tank proceeded to the end of the corridor. By the time it reached the last window of the corridor, Matties claims it was barely distinguishable from the curtains; only when they occasionally blew apart did a pale fragment of linen, a shoulder or an arm, appear. Though he climbed up on a pile of boards, Matties swore that he was unable to see the bed at the back of the room. Whatever the truth of this may have been, he could in any case not remain on the boards for long because he heard more steps coming up the drive and enter-ing the hallway.

So Erna was not with him. Pale light on the curtains and its weak reflection from the mirror like a skin eruption on the carpet. Then the weak glimmer of the brass reading-lamp on the night table and the white bedclothes of the sleeper. He was breathing evenly, an arm splayed motionless across the linen in the changing pattern of light. Had he entered a little earlier, Pnip would have seen the sleeper extend an arm and pull himself round. Pnip bent over him. The skin on the man's forehead, cheeks and neck was full of dry folds and moles. Only the narrow lipped mouth with the glittering teeth retained its tension. He had still not moved when Pnip saw a reflection in the mirror. A figure wearing his own clothes, the shoes that had stolen across the smooth parquet floor and up the stairs to the bedroom. He could see the sleeper, too, and the spot where his nipple showed through the dark silk of the pyjamas, the spot into which Pnip intended to plunge the scout knife. Pnip's breath now mixed with that of the sleeper, became heavier, louder, until only one breath could be heard in the room. Then the figure in the mirror leant back to stifle a cough and the hand on the sheet slowly contracted before it lay at peace again. Pnip again saw the mirror image crouch forward, attempt to pull the blanket aside and bare the chest for the knife. But again he hesitated. From the corner of his eye he had noticed the bare foot of the sleeper in the mirror. Now he looked at the foot itself, visible as far as the ankle and seemingly unconnected with the sleeping face. Again he bent over Glonski, his father. Now he was startled by a noise. A few seconds

113

later it came again. A smell of burning came through the open window. Then the crackling of dry wood and a sound like snow slipping off the roof. The fire leapt at the wooden wall, sucked itself in, and fanned out to produce the orange glare which, from where Pnip stood, looked like a blue-fringed, dancing flame. Glonski moved, changing the position of his arm and head. As he heaved his body round in the bed his chest passed within a hairsbreadth of Pnip's poised knife. Pnip watched it all in the mirror. Once more the glow in front of the window flared up. He must go. Heart drumming, he ran along the corridor past the now orange tinted glass. Something gave as he clambered down the stairs and out past the blazing verandah. Hawe was standing in front of the old shed wall; the shed which Glonski had preserved from the flood, against all reason. He was waving a canister over the planks. Then he struck a match and threw it on to the wall. It went up instantly, the flames mushrooming into the trees against the ink-coloured sky, frightening the birds from their perches. A pile of oil cans nourished the blaze until it blotted out the moon. And Glonski was inside. That was all; just the flames, the hiss of the wind, and the birds.

Of course I saw them coming up the drive, first one then the other. I said to myself, Matties old chap, I said, this is going to be a proper do. Then I recognized Hawe, off to the shed for his Spanish booze, I reckoned, but what's that he's carrying, I asked myself. Meanwhile the other one had got up there behind the frosted glass window, I could just make out his arm or something behind the curtains. No, Hawe was not going to the shed, he was piling up sawdust. Pouring stuff all over it, then up it went like a balloon. So that's what he's up to, I said to myself, but I didn't move. Not that I was scared of him, mind you. Though we should have had it out long ago when the wife died. Anyway, I just stood there.

That's what Matties told us when we reached the square soon after the siren had sounded. Pnip must have slipped past him just a minute or two earlier. —Bloody shed got burned down in the end without me even raising a finger. His castle, he called it. Shit to his castle, I said. Made me grovel in that bloody ditch. The filthy slavedriver. Get going, he used to shout, get that bloody saw working. Well I saw this figure up there behind the glass and then Hawe—my wife's dead, see . . .

Pnip was away now up the hill, pushing the undergrowth aside. After a while, he flung himself on the dew-wet ground, listening. Another explosion, the crackling noise carried by the wind amid the chatterings of frightened birds. Then Hawe called, running along the edge of the wood to the foot of the plantation. He kept calling but received no answer. Pnip was now bursting a pathway through the brambles with his head and shoulders. Only at the crest did he stop, just as dawn was beginning to lever the blackness of night up from the trees.

We were roused by the bell. Clara must have realized what was happening when she saw them both drive off. I've been expecting it all along, she told my uncle. She must have left the hut at once for the sirens had only just started, and she was already at Uncle's by the time I came down in my dressing gown. She barely gave us time to get dressed. In the driving mirror I saw her going on at Pomsig—now you know why I told you everything, are you listening to me? she leant forward over the seats, urging me to go faster. She didn't have to really, for we reached the sawmill before the first fire engine. The police looked a bit incredulous at first when Clara asked them to radio for tracker dogs but Matties was there to bear her out. He started rambling on again about white shirts in the window and that if need be he would have hit the intruder over the head with a club. Unfortunately, the fire had brought on an attack of high

116

blood pressure. Needless to say, he said nothing about Hawe when he talked to the police. Uncle Pomsig had borrowed a pair of rubber boots and cut himself a stick. I managed to avoid Clara but as we started up the slope she suddenly clutched my arm and asked me to help her up the hill. And so we continued with an occasional pause up the needle-covered slope.

You won't let go of me, will you?

Of course I shan't—I replied roughly. When we reached the top I caught a glimpse of the other searchers disappearing into the distance. Uncle Pomsig had dropped out. When Clara stopped, too, I presumed she was tired. But I had not reckoned with the tenacity of a desperate woman driving herself beyond exhaustion. I wanted to be free of her, to join the searchers before they caught him. What would it be like hunting someone down, with dogs, perhaps in the river, I wondered. But Clara suddenly clutched at my arm again, and dragged me down the slope we had just climbed.

Please hurry, every minute counts, she said to me.

She's just dead beat, I thought to myself, and doesn't want to admit it. Where the machine shed had stood she began running, across the clearing now flooded with water from the fire engines. Past the engines

117

towards the house. Now, she was making me really angry. She obviously thought the pace was not fast enough. I felt nauseated by the smell of the burning wreck towards which Clara was dragging me. She made her way to the cellar entrance, and started poking her umbrella against the charred door. When I reluctantly joined her, she asked me to smash the door in with my shoulder. I hesitated, then thrust myself against it. But it held firm and I felt ashamed of showing my weakness to this old woman. I tried again with the strength of injured pride, smashed a panel over the lock, thrust my hand through and released the bolt. Clara shot into the passage, stopped in front of a side door and listened. Come out—she called a little wearily. There was no need to repeat the order. A torn shirt appeared, then a soot-encrusted face, hair plastered across the forehead. With limp arms he shambled up the passage until the point of Clara's umbrella brought him to a halt. Hawe tried to form his lips into a word but produced only an unintelligible noise. Up went his arm to ward off a blow from the umbrella.

You're a good-for-nothing layabout, that's what you are! Haven't I always told you to keep your mouth shut? The umbrella rose and fell rhythmically until the idiot began to giggle, and then to run away. From one of the side rooms his laugh now echoed again as it must have done the evening before when he lay on the straw bales. Out in the yard I suddenly realized that my own fear had gone.

So they chased Pnip, with two dogs in the lead and Uncle Pomsig struggling along behind. At noon the fugitive left the plantation and led them across streams and through stunted reed grass to the Este. It was the section of the river that was filled with memories for him. Now, as he raced on, they were reduced to odd recollections—explosions in his tormented mind. There on the bank he had taken off his shorts and those white socks spotted with grass stains. Here he had dragged that black and white cat triumphantly through the water.

And here, in long trousers, he had sprawled in the grass. A motor coach had gone by, heads turned. Further down the Este, he had followed her, and then changed his mind. Later with the same girl, both lying on their backs, not daring to move closer.

The girl again, this time beneath him, her face averted. Even though the police were closer now he lingered for a moment, savouring the possibility that everything might have been otherwise. The panting of the dogs came closer. He remembered the silken mesh on her knees, her body and her hair. Only the face was missing—a pale spot with vague features that seemed unable to blend into a composite entity. But even that was enough to distract his attention from his laboured breathing and burning throat. It was enough as he ran to dream of her whose acquiescence could have changed everything.

In the afternoon his tracks became fresher and the distance between them decreased from two hours to one, and then to half an hour. The first barking of the dogs wiped out even the vaguely remembered texture of Erna's face. Again he jumped into the river and hauled himself through the reeds. As he struggled up the bank and raced across the clearing, he savoured the prospect of facing his pursuers and turning towards them.

The dogs were released. Leaping across the stream they rushed off in different directions as if chasing separate quarries, then closed in on him.

YES, he had offered to drive her home, but when he made no further move Erna started walking back alone. She passed the Huguenot villages at about midnight, and the spot where Pnip had turned round. As dawn approached she reached Gieselwerder and a truck slowly overtook her. The driver must have shouted to her for she turned her head towards the clanging of the milk churns. With his thumb he indicated that there was room for her inside. Erna sat close to him but then the pains started again, brought on by the vibration of the truck. Now she was no longer ashamed. She was a stone flung through life without a will of her own. For a man would at least have prided himself on the escape, or else have taken a passing bus to Gottsfelde or Gindenhall. But as she sat there next to the truck

121

driver Erna remained impassive. Not for her the tortured impatience of a woman on the way to meet her lover again. Of a woman impatient not so much to hold him in her arms again as to end the anxiety of waiting and the dread of the changes that come with separation.

He's called Pnip.

Never heard of him. Pnip what—Oh, I see you'd rather not tell me. But I know the one you mean. Philip Schäfer or Schröder, or something. Works in the sugar factory, doesn't he? The one that went bust the other day, so he's helping out on our farm. That's the one.

I don't think it is.

He's a fast one, that boy. Why, we had barely put the television on after tea last Saturday—Usual muck. When he was off down the village like a dose of salts. —The driver laughed and wiped his hand across his face.

Erna sat down at the kitchen table. The man placed a mug of milk and a hunk of bread before her. She felt at ease for a while, but as he called his wife in from the stables the pains came on again. She's after Philip Schröder from Schedetal he told her.

I don't think that's his name, Erna said.

The woman, her hair protruding from beneath a

headscarf, stood silently watching her. Again Erna felt it and drew her legs closer.

So that's it. Trying to find him and doesn't even know his name—said the woman suddenly. And bleeding all over the place. Take your bloody muck out of here this instant and clear off.

Cut it out, said her husband.

When they left the kitchen Erna lay down on the bench and stopped shaking. She would get there and no one would ever again need to treat her with contempt or pity. Pnip would see to it that everything was all right. From the stable came the lowing sounds of cattle. She rose quietly, slipped into the passage and let herself out. When the dog started barking, she was already walking confidently down the road. She was bound completely to her body now and to what it bore, even though she had tried to hide it in the farm. All she wanted now was to walk into the nearby town and become his wife.

Just as she saw the Gindenhall television mast appear over the top of a rise, the sirens went off. Soon afterwards she met a speeding car, followed by the first of the fire engines. Their blue lights grew bigger and bigger and then disappeared as suddenly as they had come. Now the road began to dip, to become a series of halting meanders, before straightening into a slight rise, just outside Gindenhall. Erna began to walk faster.

Certainly, the black, red, and gold flags on the courthouse were meant for an important state official and not for his benefit. But it might have seemed otherwise to the crowd that had gathered in the square to see the prisoner. In Uncle Pomsig's car I was able to force a passage to the middle of the square. Then I became trapped in the crowd which had been waiting since noon. They had first started to collect after the idiot arrived. Others quickly joined them and now, by mid-afternoon, the square was full of their low murmurings. As I watched from the roof of the car, an almost indetectable tremor seemed to run through them. In front of me, a man who could have been a teacher was holding forth, and close by on the bonnet of another car, I saw a boy who used to sit next to me at school. Brilliant at geometry he used to be. Then someone screamed and a mounted policeman with outthrust knees forced a path through the crowd. It closed immediately behind him. The noise began to swell inwards, towards the centre of the crowd. From the roof of the car I could see heads being turned towards one of the adjoining roads, slowly following a green van that was barely moving forward. They surged forward, some of them yelling:

Bastard!

Arsonist!

Murderer!

But he sat on the bunk with head erect, listening intently to their cries and yells. He revelled in their hate-filled voices, for they told him who he was at long last. Suddenly a piercing cry rang out above the general commotion. It came again. Then from where we sat we saw a seam opening in the crowd and a girl running through it towards the van. Again she called Pnip's name, then fell and was engulfed in the jeering crowd, just as the van reached the iron gates.

The next day we got the full story from Matties. The police had kept him until morning. They had questioned him about everything, his health, the death of his wife, the Yankee car and most of all about the sawmill.

So in the morning there he was in his mackintosh at Giorgio's, the only customer, tucked in behind the juke box. He chattered away and ordered another coffee but Giorgio pretended not to hear him. Giorgio had been there yesterday too; perhaps he was the one who had screamed: Communist. When Matties kept insisting, Giorgio told him the coffee machine was broken.

125

So Matties ambled off towards the Este in his rain-coat and passed the children playing hopscotch near the courthouse. It began as a muffled scraping and clattering, like stone striking stone. The girl hopped along flicking something forward with her toe. Matties watched her as he leaned against the wall of a house across the square. Slowly the children left their game and made for the prison fence. The girl started as a slate-grey shadow rose up in front of her and swooped across the street. A second pigeon followed; and still Matties did not move. He saw one of the boys link his hands together and the girl climb up, stretching as hard as she could to reach the window. For a moment she hung there, then, just as the gurgling stopped, she jumped down, panting. Only now did Matties move from the wall. The boys ran off leaving the girl at the fence gazing up at the idiot's window.

Can't you let him be, you bloody little guttersnipe, haven't they done enough to him as it is? He slapped her once or twice quite gently across the face. That same triangular face which had been greedily pressed against the window bars.

Leave him alone, for God's sake. The girl drew snot up her nose and stared at him. Old shit legs—she said and made off. Round the corner the boys were

shouting: Filthy old bastard, filthy old bastard, loves
the idiot in the cell. Then they all raced away down
the street.

But others took a different view of this episode.
Seebrecht, for one. He had been on the square too,
screaming as the van arrived. It was his stone that
had broken the prisoner's kneecap. That evening the
police brought him to the station and took a statement. Seebrecht told them that he had children but
they insisted on a reference from the polishing works.
As it turned out they did not need it nor did Uncle
Pomsig need to defend anyone. That night the idiot
hanged himself in his cell and saved all of them the
trouble. Seebrecht and the others felt guilty now, and
all he needed was to be told, when he came from the
afternoon shift at the factory:

There's another one of them about. Lucie had been
with the two baker's boys, and me always telling her,
run away if you see anyone looking funny at you.
And this one started picking on her. Wearing a
rubber coat he was, had grey hair too. I immediately
said to myself, that's the one from last spring, the
one who was in the papers, blow me if he isn't. . . .

A rubber coat, eh?

Yes, and grey hair. Always run away, Lucie, that's
what I told her.

Later, when they sat at Giorgio's, Seebrecht was telling them about the stone. I was only holding it in my palm, he said, so why the hell do they want a statement or my driving licence. Call that democracy —and so on.

The others were silent, for though they, too, had screamed in the square, they all felt embarrassed now. That's why they said nothing when Seebrecht went rambling on about the rubber coat and Matties being crazy. I was sitting next to one of them beside the juke box. The differential calculus was again giving me trouble and had already cost me two packets of cigarettes. Suddenly one of them called across from two tables away and asked me about Clara. Giorgio stopped washing up. What was I to tell them? That I had seen her prodding the charred door with her umbrella? How the idiot eventually came out? So I was glad when they noticed Matties coming slowly up the street past the papershop and the iron-monger's. Outside, the traffic had grown noisier, but not noisy enough to drown the whistle of the polishing works. Another shift had ended. Cars, scooters and bicycles were again flooding into the town. The deluge of traffic that had swept Pnip past the out-skirts of the town. Now, as the days were drawing in, the sunlight flickering on this river of traffic looked muted. It was the sunlight of early autumn, and that night there was the chance of ground frost. I thought of yesterday's riot in the square, the screams, and the police van ploughing its way into the crowd. The memory of it all was sharp, or else it was the frozen tableau I could see through the open door—a traffic jam, a lorry crawling along, then a cyclist balancing —that drove home to me the uneasy conscience of the town.

As I told you, we heard about it because Matties wouldn't keep his mouth shut. He had sat down close to the door beneath an open window. Perhaps he had been searching all day for someone to listen to his story. For although Seebrecht jumped up, shouting about rubber-coated perverts, and wanted to beat him up, and though his coffee never came, Matties went on and on. Tell me what you would have done in my place, he said. The fellow comes up to me just as I am going to top a few beet. Working extra fast, too, I was, because Rose had been complaining. But there he was beside me and me trying not to listen to a word he says.

I could still manage the beet as well as the next man. So why should I have listened to him, how the hell could he have known anyway? But he kept repeating his story. I started hacking more quickly now, Rosie

129

had told me yesterday to get them done. Then he grabbed me by the arm and yelled into my ear, so I had to listen. There were the beet, but what could I do? No more topping today, I said to myself, that's for sure.

Where is my coffee, I ordered it hours ago. Seebrecht started about Lucie again but Magosch shut him up. Magosch had laughed when his boys had told him about Matties's outburst outside the prison. Someone mentioned Yanks, and Giorgio asked if the fellow was a communist, and about the time when the Werra bridge was smashed and the big Yankee lorries had to climb up the slope. Took a long time to pick up speed again at the top, they did, Matties explained. So slow you could easily creep up. One had overturned on the hill. Coffee was everywhere and the people from Laubach were grubbing away at it while a G.I. stood there laughing himself silly. He was even showing them a couple of bags they had missed. Matties, I thought, there's something here for you. The Yank was probably still laughing when he was miles away and telling himself what a generous bastard he was. There's the place, I thought, no Yankees about and you can get right up to the lorries. One came alone, the Negro driving it threw me a piece of chocolate. Nice fellow, I thought and stuffed

130

it in my pocket. Better let him go by. Then a jeep
came along and I cleared off. That lot saw me with
the Negro, I said to myself, and they're spoiling for
trouble. Then another one came along. A German,
this time, spluttering like hell on its wood-burning
engine. Then another Yank. You're in luck, Matties,
this one's got guns or cans on board, I said to myself.
Six wheeler, too, going to be a job getting that rope
off the tarpaulin. It was packed jam-tight with boxes.
Must get them off before the bastard speeds up over
the top. I threw the boxes down the slope, at least
ten of them. You're in luck, Matties, I told myself,
Bismarck herrings, corned beef and dried milk. One
had a picture of a leg of mutton on it. And cartons of
Pall Mall and Chesterfield. Come back tomorrow
with Fiedler's horse. Tell him I want to get some top-
soil. But it's steep going to Laubach, and the beast
wouldn't go up, bit my arm, the bastard did. While I
was still racking my brains for a way out, I saw a
lorry coming up the hill with a trailer, so I quickly
hid the horse, and rifled that one instead. All was
quiet while I started loading the cart. Only my arm
hurt where the bastard of a horse had bitten me. Two
more boxes and off we go, I thought. But just then
another jeep had to come up the hill. He's stopped at
the top, the sun reflecting from his windscreen,

131

while I dived behind a bush. When I got back at last, I couldn't believe my eyes, for the bloody thing had gone, and I had tethered the beast securely. No horse, no cart. So I stood there like an idiot with three boxes. I could see the tracks with the sun shining on them. But that was all.

What about the fire, Matties, Magosch asked quickly. And which of the two got into the bedroom?

Did you actually see—said the man next to me, but Matties could not be stopped now. He had been searching all day for someone to listen to his story. Now he sat fumbling with his rubber coat, just missing the button holes with his thick fingers. His eyes were inflamed from yesterday's fire or perhaps from the night's watch. But as he looked up, I noticed they were calm and peaceful. He was just unlucky, I thought, let himself be tricked and he knows it.— The horse must have bolted and got jammed in the trees. What will I tell Fiedler? Then I saw the tracks continue beyond the trees and on to the road, and felt sure the bloody horse was going to drag the whole lot into town. They won't be able to stop it either, I thought. It will bolt down the High Street, smash the cart against a wall and send all my loot flying. So I ran as fast as I could and everyone yelled what's wrong. Don't worry, I shouted back but I might as

well have saved my breath for there was nothing for
them to get worried about. Not a trace anywhere. I'll
have to tell Fiedler that the axle's broken and that he
can have the bloody cart back tomorrow, I said to
myself. Then I pinched a bicycle and beat it to Gottsfelde. I kept thinking about Fiedler and axles and
tomorrow and I didn't know what to do. Best to get
busy with the beets again. Finish the lot by evening.
They were good that year, like honey, if only the cart
hadn't disappeared. Suddenly he was beside me, talking away. I ignored him and kept on chopping, I just
didn't want to hear. Why can't you let me alone with
the beets, I thought. But he kept on at me and
grabbed my arm. What do you want, I said, leave me
alone. Next thing I knew he was dragging me across
the field. And there was Fiedler's horse and cart with
the boxes on it. Put them in your cellar, he said. And
make sure your wife keeps her mouth shut, do you
understand? And what could I do? He said he saw
me jumping on the lorry, then hiding after the Negro
gave me that piece of chocolate. In fact he saw everything. You let one lorry pass, he said, then fleeced
the next one. If only I had stayed with my beet as
Rosie told me to. Now, I was stuck with a bloody
madman, for that's what he was. Drew a plan of a
new shed in the sand; you're crazy, I kept telling him,

133

and scattered it with my feet. So he went for me, knew I was past it, the bloody slavedriver. Rosie stood there in the doorway watching it all. Should have stayed with my beets. Christ, he was ranting now but I'd had about enough, too. Up with the shovel, but all he said was, one blow with that and you'll be in jail for life. It was enough for me. Even when he started on my pet bantam, I couldn't do anything. Lovely bird, it was, white with a red comb and what a fighter. Only had one eye, left the other in Hämer's yard that time when he finished off a Rhode Islander. Well, that day he was leading his hens across the yard. Across Glonski's precious drawing. It wasn't badly smudged so I said, what the hell. But I could see Glonski was furious. Next morning they'd been at it again, and I thought, well Matties I thought, there's going to be trouble. That afternoon Glonski was nailing new roofing felt on to the shed—he was the only one who could get it in those days, God knows how. Got rid of all my loot, too, and used the proceeds to buy old machines. Anyway, he was up there on the shed hammering away for all he was worth. The cock fluttered up and started pecking away at the roofing felt, you know, the one with the single eye. No hens with him today. He came closer looking for caterpillars no doubt, found something and started pecking away at it. Glonski went for him like a bomb. Next thing you know, he has kicked the poor beast down the bloody roof. The cock struggled to get up to the top again, but Glonski was after him with the hammer. The first blow missed, just caught the poor beast's foot. Rosie was behind me, shaking with fright. Break his neck if you must, I yelled, but not like that, not with the hammer. Now he was fluttering down the roof, squawking like crazy. Glonski was still taking cracks at him, but couldn't finish him off properly. Rosie had started screaming by then and I thought, what sort of filthy business is this. Then at last Glonski crushed the poor bugger's skull. Yes, I see, said Magosch treating him like an idiot, pity about the eye, still, have a brandy on me. That's the way, I thought, turn him into an idiot and write him off that way now that they can't pin this business of Seebrecht's daughter on to him. Turn him into an idiot and make a fool of him as Glonski did. And he was certainly an embarrassment to them. Even I had heard their hideous screams as the police van forced its way through them, and as the girl fell down among them. All they wanted was to drag the prisoner out of the van, and to hell with the girl. Then I saw a figure in a rubber coat leap out, thrust his shoulder against the crowd, as solid as a

135

door, and plough through them like a blade. He pressed on to the place where the girl lay. The van had now passed through the prison gate which was quickly bolted behind it. Perhaps it was the action of this rubber-coated figure in charging through the crowd— in any case the crowd stopped surging against the prison fence and the courthouse with its black, red and yellow flag. Now they were swaying uncertainly. A single blast of a hooter, or the cry of a blackbird as it passed over the square would have been enough to send them off in another direction. As it was they stood about the square while Matties lifted the girl into his arms. She slipped from his grasp and fell once more to the ground. He bent over her.

One of them, is she? a voice jeered. And then. Look the old idiot's crying.

Yes, I thought to myself, you all remember what the old man in the rubber coat was doing while you were screaming and throwing stones. So you have to turn him into an idiot and talk to him as if he were a child. But the worst part of it was that he did not even notice. Again they questioned him, eager to know more about last night. He was good enough for that. But he wanted to tell them the whole story from the beginning and not just the one bit they wanted to hear.

—So I knew the slavedriver was mad, but how could I know that what he was mad for was a son? That's why I never thought that Rosie . . . Well there I was without my chickens and all my beet going to waste. He made me saw all day long, for Glonski could get timber when others couldn't even get firewood. Matties, I said to myself, he's really got you sewn up. Rosie is so silent these days, what can be the matter with her, I thought. Getting old, makes them all strange. Why does the slavedriver have to stand so close to me all the time? If only I hadn't gone after those boxes at Laubach. Now my farm is gone, and my cockerel, and Rosie's getting queerer every day. Change of life, that's what's making her behave so strangely. For the rest everything seemed fine between us. That's why I kept quiet, though everyone said I was a fool. Yes, I know you do, too. But you don't know the half of it—about Laubach and the way he got his machines, I mean. God, what can be wrong with her, what's the matter with her, look at her, she must be getting old. But now her apron was tightening and I wondered, could it be possible? She said not to worry, so what could I do but go away and saw all day long. Sawing all the time. Perhaps it's her change of life, after all, anyway she said it was. It had to be, no one could do this

137

to me. Always behind me driving me on, boards and sawdust all day long. I thought to myself, I'd like to saw his bloody head off. But he had me just where he wanted. It all rushed through my brain, her change of life, that's right, husband, she told me, so what could I do but get back to my logs? What else had I left, no beet, no property, just sawing boards in the sunlight, and even the sun didn't warm me any more. So I started crying, didn't know what else to do. Just standing there at my wits' end and howling.

If only they would leave him in peace, I thought, but they kept on with their questions. Giorgio, give him another coffee, he can do with one. Yes, I thought, they'll buy him a coffee, and then go off again, calling him an idiot, and expecting him to be grateful.

Well, we'd lost two sons, and her change of life is coming, best leave her alone, I told myself. I knew the slavedriver was mad for a son. And Rosie was mad for one too, it's coming in the spring, she told me, but there's nothing for you to worry about. And when spring came, there I was sitting in the doorway with my hands over my ears to shut out her groans. The one day he was needed, and the bastard was away buying new machines. It was spring and I was thinking of beet. Rosie was there. The earth was soft, Christ, you could dig your fingers in it. Grab a handful of it and snatch the leaves from the beech tree and chew them. Roll them in your mouth, then spit them out before they turn too bitter, it really does you good. I could see the sun above the trees, see-sawing in the boughs. Really enjoying himself up there. In front of me a blackbird jabbed into the ground, tugged away and pulled up a big worm. Made for the beech tree, wiped its beak then came down again. It's spring, it must have said to itself, so why are there so few worms? But after a while, finding nothing but sawdust, it clears off. Matties, old chap, I said, you've got diarrhoea and its gone terribly quiet inside the house. Then her pains really started. She was sweating and threshing about now and cursing the slavedriver for all she was worth. I couldn't very well tell her that he had gone for the day, so I said he's coming back any minute. Christ, her screams, I could barely stand them. Curse the bastard, my wife is an old woman. He's on the way, I kept telling her, but of course he was miles away getting machines. In the end, I set off for the village, diarrhoea and all. The ground was soft as I ran. He's done for you, Matties. Midwife says she is coming but she's so old and so slow. Better stay outside, she said when she arrived at long last. So I waited just where the beet used to be. Screaming now, she was, so I ran back, thinking it can't be long now. The door was shut. Matties, she screamed, but it was the slave-driver she really wanted, not me. It was he who trod her, he who sired Pnip and Klaus. And now that she needed him, the sod had gone for machines. Suddenly she stopped screaming in there. I was sweating now, God, how wet the earth was. You could thrust your whole arm into it. Right up to the wrist. When she screamed again, half my forearm was in. I pushed away till my arm was near breaking. Then I jerked it out of the earth. When the old midwife came to the door, I didn't have to ask, for I knew it all anyway. Yes, the slavedriver had another son and my wife was dead.

That one over there, the one by the juke box, Klaus, the one who lives with that slimy twister, Pomsig, he came out on his bicycle. Asking if Glonski was his father. As if he didn't know from Pomsig, Uncle Pomsig he calls him. Brainy boy, though he looks a bloody fool. Still going to college and talking fancy. Talk straight, I said, or shut your mouth.

Of course I'm fond of him and I was fond of Hawe too. Clara's boy, Pnip, as well. True, it was him I saw up there in his old man's bedroom, but he didn't start it all the same. I like the whole rotten bunch of them as if they were my own. Just listen, that little squirt with his smart questions wants to write about it when he is older. Always asking about Pnip and Hawe. So I told him there's Pnip, there's Hawe, and you came in the middle. Now scram or I'll kick your stupid head in. That shocked him but then I had to grin a little and he saw it. Back he came. You're crazy, I told him, just piss off.

A Note about the Author

Peter Faecke was born in 1940 as the 501st in-
habitant of a Silesian village near the Czech border
where his father was a forester. In 1945 his family
moved to Lower Saxony, where young Faecke at-
tended school. He was graduated from the University
of Göttingen with a degree in German and Romance
Languages and Literature and continued his studies
in Berlin, Hamburg, and Paris. His first novel, *The
Firebugs,* was published in Germany in 1963 and was
soon scheduled for translation into English, French,
Swedish, Italian, Spanish, and Danish.

July 1965

A Note on the Type

The text of this book was set on the Linotype in a face called TIMES ROMAN, designed by Stanley Morison for The Times (London), and first introduced by that newspaper in 1932.

Among typographers and designers of the twentieth century, Stanley Morison has been a strong forming influence, as typographical advisor to the English Monotype Corporation, as a director of two distinguished English publishing houses, and as a writer of sensibility, erudition, and keen practical sense.

Printed in offset by Halliday Lithograph Corp., West Hanover, Mass. Bound by The Book Press, Brattleboro, Vt.